Sue MacKay lives with her husband in New Zealand's beautiful Marlborough Sounds, with the water on her doorstep and the birds and the trees at her back door. It is the perfect setting to indulge her passions of entertaining friends by cooking them sumptuous meals, drinking fabulous wine, going for hill walks or kayaking around the bay—and, of course, writing stories.

Also by Sue MacKay

A December to Remember
Breaking All Their Rules
Dr White's Baby Wish
The Army Doc's Baby Bombshell
Resisting Her Army Doc Rival
Pregnant with the Boss's Baby
Falling for Her Fake Fiancé
Her New Year Baby Surprise
Baby Miracle in the ER
Surprise Twins for the Surgeon

Discover more at millsandboon.co.uk.

ER DOC'S FOREVER GIFT

SUE MacKAY

MILLS & BOON

First published in Great Britain 2018
by Mills & Boon, an imprint of HarperCollins*Publishers*
1 London Bridge Street, London, SE1 9GF

Large Print edition 2019

© 2018 Sue MacKay

ISBN: 978-0-263-07826-8

MIX
Paper from
responsible sources
FSC™ C007454

This book is produced from independently certified FSC™ paper to ensure responsible forest management. For more information visit www.harpercollins.co.uk/green.

Printed and bound in Great Britain
by CPI Group (UK) Ltd, Croydon, CR0 4YY

To all those amazing people who fly the rescue helicopters and to the medical personnel on board, whether in easy situations or dangerous locations.
You rock.

CHAPTER ONE

LIFE COULD BE so damned unfair.

There were days Sienna Burch hated being a paediatrician, today being one of them. Maybe she should bow out at the end of her contract, go buy a patch of land in a sleepy backwater and grow tomatoes and wear a long, billowy skirt.

Like hell.

While colleagues had warned her she'd been on a hiding to nowhere from the moment young Caleb was admitted with meningitis, she also knew parents trusted her to do all she could for their adored child. She always did that. But they also expected her to win, and unfortunately, that outcome wasn't achievable every single time.

Another yawn pulled at her. It would be too easy to shuffle further down the SUV's seat and drop into a deep sleep right here in her garage. Far too effortless. Elbowing the door open, she gathered her handbag and jacket up from the passenger seat before staggering upright.

Bed? Or food? She needed both. And a shower. Food took time because she'd have to clean up afterwards. Unless she went for the easy, not so healthy option of a toasted sandwich and only one pan to rinse out. There was ham and cheese in the fridge. Her tongue lapped her lips. Yes, she did allow herself a few semi-healthy treats. Sighing, she headed for the kitchen, flicked on lights, dropped the blind.

Boom, boom, boom.

'What the—?' Music loud enough to wake the dead thumped through the walls. 'Great. Why tonight?'

The new guy next door nearly always had music of some genre on the go when he was at home, but rarely was it loud and intrusive. In the living room she flicked on more lights. Hopefully he'd notice she was home and cut the volume. That was when she heard laughter and voices. 'He's having a party. Wonderful.' How did that happen when he was new in town on a temporary contract at the Rescue Helicopter base, temporarily replacing her real neighbour for three months?

Not that Sienna had met the guy, only caught a couple of glances of a well-honed body filling out jeans in a way that should have him a modelling contract with the manufacturers. Not her type at all. *Oh, yeah, then what is?* With her crazy schedule she rarely had civilised hours to have fun in.

The guy seldom seemed to be home either. Not unless he liked permanently closed windows and doors. Another blast of music slapped her. If only he had the place shut up tight tonight. How was she going to sleep with that going on?

Forget toasting a sandwich. Bread and cheese while tugging clothes off and getting under the shower was the way to go. Her bed was beckoning with relentless persistence. Only thing was, her mind couldn't blank out the anguished cries of Caleb's parents as they'd switched off life support. From past experience she knew there were no shortcuts getting through this anguish, that it took time and looking after herself—which meant getting adequate sleep.

Thump, thump, thump. And she'd thought

the volume was at its max. Sliding right down her bed, covers up to her neck, pillow over her head, Sienna closed her eyes and counted sheep. Not that those dumb animals ever helped her out, but she needed to zone out, find oblivion.

Then her dad piped up in the fog filling her head. Of course he did.

'Relax. Enjoy life and all it's got to offer. What's happened to my girl who loved to track butterflies? Who wanted to grow wings and fly?'

His words taunted her whenever she was too tired to fight them.

'Not tonight, Dad. Please.'

An hour later, Sienna tossed the pillow and covers aside to swing her legs out of bed. The headache pills she'd taken with her bread were not working as the drums in her head were louder and harsher than ever. Those weren't the worst beats. Next door there had to be a whole band of drummers competing with each other; the noise level was so unbelievably high. The voices had also increased in volume.

All she wanted was eight hours straight being comatose. Hours where Caleb didn't feature, where his parents' sobs didn't break her heart. Hours in which she couldn't think about her promise to her father to lighten up some by Christmas. She'd settled here, in this city, bought this apartment for a reason and nothing or no one could be allowed to change it. Yet it seemed everyone was trying to.

Click, click. Her vertebrae pulled her straight. Time to confront her neighbour. Her muscles began to soften. She didn't do conflict, unless she was fighting for a patient's life. Yes, well, her patients needed her to get some sleep so she could think straight. *Click, click.* That music was going to shut down. Now.

Harry sat on the edge of the deck, a warming bottle of beer swinging from his fingers. Midnight had been and gone. If only he could say the same for his visitors. Unfortunately they all seemed intent on burying their raw grief in loud music and lots of shouting and talking.

A tight-knit group, they'd naturally turned to each other today when they heard the news of the loss of their top pilot after the helicopter he was flying back from having the machine serviced went out of control and hit the ground.

The cause of the crash was as yet unknown, and likely to be for weeks, if not months, but the mechanics were on high alert. Bet the crews would be too, come tomorrow.

Lights came on in the apartment next door, then the deck was flooded in a yellow glow.

Oh, oh. Trouble on the horizon? Harry shrugged and sipped the beer, not really enjoying it yet reluctant to set it aside. His hands always had to be busy. If only he had something to do to fill in the hours before this lot were ready to head home in the taxis he'd order, and pay for. Being the new boy on the block, he hadn't known Gavin Bradley well, but the guy was a legend in the emergency air service—his reputation for spot-on retrieval in difficult conditions ran the length of the country. He would be missed very much.

A shadow crossed the end of the drive, turned in his direction. The shadow became human, walking with confidence and yet at the same time almost with caution, like a young girl with little care to burden her. Then she came into the light, making her way up towards him, an opposing grim expression on what might be a beautiful face if she wasn't carrying the weight of the world on her back. Apparently this was the girl next door. Only he could see now her girl days were long gone, morphed into someone who stole the breath away from him and tightened his groin without any input from his brain.

Harry slowly drew another mouthful of beer—it really was foul—and put the bottle down on the deck beside him. 'Hello. So we finally get to meet.'

That delicious mouth flattened further. 'This is not a social call.' Her voice was husky—and laden with barely contained anger.

'That's a shame.' In more ways than he cared to admit, even to himself. Close up, she was even better looking than he'd first thought. Her flawless skin covered perfect facial bone structure. 'I'm Harry, by the way.'

That startled her. 'Sienna Burch,' she snapped. Hadn't she expected to be introducing herself?

'So what can I do for you, Sienna?' Though he kind of had an idea what was getting her knickers in a twist. It was late on a working night, and the guys inside were a little loud.

'Could you please turn the music down? Or preferably off? I need to get some sleep.' Her expression wasn't softening, but that didn't quieten his pulse. A bit of a challenge in the making?

Over the past weeks he'd been vaguely aware of her coming and going at all hours, but hadn't got around to introducing himself. Nothing unusual in that when he was on a short stint in a town he was unlikely to return to. His breath caught. He had to be slipping—because behind whatever was tightening her face this particular woman was a stunner, and he was partial to stunners. Fess up, he liked women, full stop. Especially hot, shapely, downright beautiful ones. If that made him shallow then he could live with that. It suited his mantra: keep moving on.

'Excuse me. The music?'

'I'll give it a go, certainly.' Now he could hear one of the girls crying behind him. That'd been a while coming. Apart from initial tears everyone had been stoic, but he'd known it was only a matter of time before they showed their grief in the teary form. And he was supposed to charge in and turn the music off and make like everyone should go home?

'I'd prefer that you actually did it, not make a half-hearted attempt. I've had a long, difficult day and I need to sleep.'

Bet your day was a breeze compared to the one these guys are dealing with.

'I'm sorry about that. I will do my best, but I have to warn you my colleagues are suffering an enormous shock and this is their way of letting off steam.' It wasn't as though he had the sound turned up to full volume every night of the week. This was a one-off.

That tight mouth wasn't giving an inch. 'I see.'

No, she didn't. 'Have you seen the news today?'

'As if.' Finally that mouth softened a fraction, and Sienna lifted her chin slightly. Definitely beautiful in a classic way. 'What did I miss?'

'One of the rescue helicopters went down this morning.'

She gasped. Now that tightness was taking a backward step. 'With serious consequences I take it.'

'The pilot died and the other pilot on board is in a serious condition in the ICU at Auckland

Hospital. Fortunately they didn't have medical crew or a patient on board or there'd be more casualties.'

Another gasp, and Sienna moved closer. 'I'm sorry. That's terrible. I didn't hear about that.'

What did she do for a living? Take gym classes in a cave? That tee shirt and those fitted leggings highlighted a well-formed body with muscles in the right places and soft curves to add a sensuality that teased him. Like he needed this right now. But it seemed certain parts of his body were out of sync with the sadness roiling in his mind. *They* wanted action. *They* weren't getting any.

Then Sienna added, 'I'm sorry to hear that. Really sorry.' Another step and she was beside the deck.

'It's been a huge shock for everyone. You understand I'm filling in at the helicopter rescue service?'

'Yes.' She leaned her tidy butt against the handrail post. 'I haven't been very neighbourly, but I'm hardly ever at home.'

'Don't worry about it. I'll be gone in a month.'

Sienna straightened again. 'Anyway, I do

need to get some shut-eye. My day wasn't a lot better.'

Her frostiness did nothing to detract from her looks, but however much she needed some quiet his loyalties lay with those inside his apartment. 'Maybe, but I'm giving these people the chance to de-stress before making sure they get home safely. You could join us and wind down from whatever upset you with a wine and some music.'

'It would take a lot more than that.'

He had to ask. 'What happened?' Damn it, why couldn't he just mind his own business? Now he'd have to listen to some story that barely registered compared to the crash, as well as be sympathetic.

'I lost a patient. A six-year-old boy.' Her bottom lip trembled.

Damned if he didn't want to haul her into his arms and hold her until the trembling stopped. His fingers gripped the beer bottle as if his life depended on it. 'That's terrible. You're a doctor?' Not a gym instructor, then.

'A paediatrician. The best, and the worst, job out there.' Her voice was low and slow.

She's a doctor?

That explained the hours she was away from home. Who'd have thought it? But then, why not?

We don't all come with labels on our foreheads proclaiming our medical knowledge. And why can't doctors be beautiful, and have stunning figures?

Just because he'd never met one quite as attractive as Sienna Burch, didn't mean they didn't exist.

Then she yawned.

Which got to him, made him want to soothe her to sleep. 'The kids are the worst cases. They always get to me, even if only for a greenstick fracture.'

'And the parents. They're hurting as bad. They want to take the pain into themselves so their babies don't have to suffer, and it's torture when they can't.' Sienna lifted her head and stared at him, her own pain obvious.

She took her job seriously, but it was hard to find a good doctor who didn't. Impossible. Thoughtlessly he reached across with one hand to touch her arm. So much for hanging on to his bottle as a shield. 'I totally understand.' Squeezing lightly, he hurriedly pulled away.

But it was too late. Warmth trickled from her skin through his fingers and up his arm.

Sienna was upright—and uptight. 'If you can't turn the music off then at least lower the decibels.'

Sarah, one of the pilots, appeared on the deck. 'I think everyone's ready to head home now.'

Harry stood up and found his neighbour's head came up to his chin. Not often that happened. 'There you go. You should be able to get that kip soon.'

'I appreciate it.' Sienna turned and stumbled down the path, not so youthful in her movements now.

He couldn't take his eyes off her. Somehow she'd woven her way under his skin while being the antithesis of the open, cheery women he usually went for. She hadn't effused sympathy, nor had she been cold about what had happened, just contained. But then, she was used to other people's pain. 'See you,' he called after her, the temptation to goad her just a little way too hard to ignore. If she could shake him up, then he could return the favour. 'Maybe we'll both be at home at the same time one night this week.' Unlikely since he was rarely here and then mostly only to eat and sleep.

There was no reply, just a lengthening of the strides taking her away.

As he was unused to being ignored, his interest was piqued. Had it been entirely her bad day at work putting that exhaustion in her face, her eyes? Or was there more going on in her life causing problems? Harry huffed a bitter breath. Why did he even want to know? He didn't do getting to know women beyond the obvious, yet within minutes Sienna Burch had got under his skin like a serious itch. Not a good look. Best he didn't scratch. That was going to take some serious effort, for sure.

'I'll start ordering taxis, shall I?' Sarah nudged his arm with her shoulder. 'For most of this lot anyway.'

Sarah had been trying to get his attention, as in up close and personal, from the day he'd started at the rescue service, and he'd been putting out the thanks-but-no-thanks signal to no avail. It would do wonders for his tired soul to lose himself in a woman tonight. Which was blatantly on offer, if he was reading Sarah correctly, and he had no reason to think otherwise.

But he had a hard and fast rule—no sex with colleagues.

Sienna isn't a colleague.

His gaze tripped sideways to the other drive leading up to the adjacent apartment and the woman stepping onto an identical front step. Short-tempered, not overly concerned for others needing an outlet for their grief, a different kind of woman. Intriguing. Irritating. To be ignored, forgotten about. If that was possible. *It had better be.* He turned to his co-worker. 'Make sure everyone gets a ride home. Everyone,' he repeated in case his message hadn't got through. Boy, wouldn't he like to scratch that itch with Sienna.

His temporary neighbour had ruffled his feathers. He couldn't remember the last time a female had done that. Probably when he was fifteen and keen for just about any girl willing to join him in a bit of fun. His gaze remained on the neighbouring apartment, noting lights turning off, another going on—in the bedroom. Bedroom, bed, sheets, or not. Go, damn it. Just focus on that temporary bit and he'd be fine, wouldn't succumb to the sudden craving filling him.

I won't. I really won't.

Would he? Could he call her a colleague because they were both doctors? It'd be a stretch but something to hang on to if this itch got too strong.

CHAPTER TWO

'WE'VE LANDED ON the roof of the hospital, Felicity,' Harry told his young patient. 'You'll soon be inside where the doctors can take good care of you.' He checked the belts holding her on the stretcher.

She pushed the face mask aside. 'I don't want to be here. I wanted to stay on the island.' Petulance didn't suit her.

Gently putting the mask back in place, he said in his best friendly doctor voice, 'You need checking out by the specialists.' He could understand that petulance but she'd nearly drowned. With lungs in the condition of hers because of the cystic fibrosis, that was bad. 'You coughed up a lot of water.'

The mask was again shoved away. 'You don't get it,' griped the fifteen-year-old. 'This was the end-of-year trip that all year tens in science have been slogging their guts out for. Me included. And on the first day you bring me back to Auckland. Thanks a bundle.'

His heart softened for this angry girl. People with her condition didn't get a fair bat at life. But as a doctor there was no way he could've left her on Great Barrier Island. They might've cleared the water from her lungs, but all of it? Secondary drowning was always a risk, especially with her condition. Close attention was required for the next twenty-four hours.

'Ready?' asked Connor, his off-sider, standing on the ground waiting to take one end of the stretcher.

'Sure am.' Harry nodded to Felicity. 'I'm sorry I had to bring you home.'

She blinked and tears spurted out of the corners of her eyes. 'It's not your fault. I shouldn't blame you. If Tony Wilcox hadn't leapt on my back I wouldn't have gone under water. *I* know not to. At least not for as long as I was down there. I got stuck on a rocky ledge for a bit.'

Again he replaced the mask, certain she'd remove it any minute. 'You give him a hard time when you both get back to school.' With practised ease he and Connor quickly had the stretcher out and rolling towards the sliding door decorated with red and gold tinsel that gave access to the hospital emergency lift. Staff in scrubs were waiting for them. Presumably a doctor and nurses. Wait. The serious demeanour on one face was familiar. The slam as his stomach hit his toes was not. 'Sienna? You work at Auckland Central?' Duh, obviously. It made sense, given that she lived not too far away.

An abrupt nod in his direction as though he was immaterial to this scene had his blood more than heating—it was boiling. Down, boy. Not the time or place. For confrontation, or getting friendly. What was it with her that already his body was reacting so blatantly? She really had worked a number on him. Bet she had no idea either. Damn it.

'Hi, Fliss. This is a bummer, isn't it?' Sienna was focusing on their patient almost as if she hadn't acknowledged him while everyone prepared to transfer the girl over to the hospital bed and change oxygen supplies.

'It's not fair, is what it is,' grizzled the once again maskless girl. 'You told me I'd be all right for a few days, Doc Sienna.'

'I'm sorry, Fliss, I guess I was wrong.' Nothing but compassion in her voice.

Sienna was taking the blame for something that was totally out of her control? Miss—make that Dr—Frosty? He really had read her all wrong last week. Or was it only in her medical capacity she managed to show warmth towards others? 'I take it Felicity's a regular patient of yours?' Harry looked to Sienna.

'Yes. We've been working towards this stay on the island for weeks now.'

Sympathy radiated out of those eyes he now saw were vivid blue, the colour of Lake Tekapo on a summer's day. A lake he'd spent a day on trying to catch trout the first time he worked in New Zealand. It had been a fantastic day and despite the lack of fish he'd never forgotten how relaxed the stunning mountainous scenery and the bouncing waters had made him feel. It was a place he intended to revisit, if he ever found himself with a couple of spare days. The lake would be warmer than Sienna was towards him. Why the chill? Could that explain this overreaction to her? She was a challenge? It couldn't be that he wanted to get to know her better, except maybe physically, and by the steely glint in those eyes *that* wasn't happening.

'Can I have the notes?' A hand with rose-pink, perfectly manicured nails highlighting long, slim fingers waved in front of him.

Harry shook his head to rid the thoughts his overheated brain conjured up of those nails tripping over his hot skin. This was his unfriendly neighbour. Doc Frosty would never be interested in running her fingers anywhere near him. Not unless she was going to use them to impale him for not turning down the music the moment she'd requested he do so. The following morning she'd barely managed a nod in his direction as she'd left for work when he'd gone out to the four-wheel-drive that came with the apartment.

'Excuse me, the notes?'

Focus, man. Passing over the required information, he explained, 'The school first-aid officer managed to get Felicity to bring up a lot of water before we arrived, but she's still coughing up fluid intermittently.' A lot of that had to do with the mucus clogging her lungs, but still there was danger in residual salt water wreaking havoc with her breathing.

'I'm glad the first-aid officer knew what to do.' The frost melted a little as she studied Felicity.

'I agree.' Harry nodded before filling Sienna in on more details. Then he crossed to Felicity. 'You take care, now; get back on your feet quick smart. Don't let Tony Wilcox win this one.' He got a watery smile in return.

'Who's Tony Wilcox?' Doc Frosty asked from right beside him in a not so chilly tone.

'The guy who caused Felicity to have her head under water too long.'

'He didn't mean it,' their patient interjected, with a red flush going on in her cheeks.

So that was how this went. Young Felicity was keen on Tony and didn't want to show it. 'I'm sure he didn't.' Harry grinned, then turned to Sienna, his mouth still curved upward. 'Might see you later, Doctor.'

As in, I could drop in to your place with a bottle of wine.

And probably get thrown out on his butt, because that had to be the dumbest idea he'd had in a long time.

Once again he didn't get any acknowledgement from Sienna as she headed into the lift, all her attention on their patient. He couldn't fault her for that. Felicity came first, but it irked that she hadn't taken a few seconds to give him a nod. Yet the woman had apologised to her young patient for her trip going horribly wrong. The doc did have a heart. She might keep it buried deep, but he certainly couldn't fault her for that. He did the same. It saved getting too involved and then having to bail when things got too intense. But still, he wouldn't have minded a smile: a warm, tender one like the smile she had for her patient.

Sienna held her breath until the door to the lift closed off the view of her neighbour. Her *very sexy* neighbour. It didn't make sense. Harry wore red one-size-fits-most overalls and he looked hot beyond belief. There again, she'd been out of the dating circuit for years so could be that a four-foot-nothing, overweight goat would look sexy in the right circumstances.

A hand was tugging at her sleeve. Drawing in air and shutting out Harry, she turned to her patient. 'Hey, Fliss, I hear you took seawater on board. That won't make your lungs happy.'

The face mask was snatched away and words

spewed out. 'It's not fair. I worked so hard to go on the trip. It's the first time Mum's let me go away without her and now I'll be a prisoner in my own home again.'

'Put this back on.' As the lift jerked downward Sienna slipped the mask over Felicity's face.

It was promptly torn off. 'Why bother? I don't have a life anyway. Not one I like.' Tears were tracking down her sallow cheeks as she gasped in tight lungfuls of air. Short, sharp gasps that wouldn't give her anywhere near enough oxygen. 'What happens if I don't get home for Christmas, huh?'

To run with the physical problem, or the real issue behind this? Like other children with cystic fibrosis, Felicity had missed out on a lot over the years. 'Your mum only wants what's best for you.' Sienna drew a breath. Yvonne Little also had a son with the same condition and was raising the children on her own, her husband having thrown in the towel saying he couldn't cope. As if Yvonne cruised through everything. 'I know you want more than anything to be doing what your friends are, but we both understand that's not always possible.'

'Doesn't mean I have to like it.'

'No, it doesn't. As for Christmas, you'll be home well before then.' Fliss could also be back in here with yet another of the massive chest infections she was prone to, but Sienna wasn't bringing up that subject. The girl knew it as well as she did.

'My grandparents are coming in two weeks. I don't want to be in here then.'

This discussion could go round and round endlessly. Sienna gave her a smile. 'Let's get you cleaned up, and start monitoring your obs. If everything's all right, you should be able to go home tomorrow.' She'd been about to say 'go back to Great Barrier Island' but realised in the nick of time it wasn't her place, that Yvonne didn't need her adding to her problems.

'Whatever.' Felicity tugged the mask back over her face, closed her eyes and turned her shoulder towards Sienna.

Sienna made a mental note to talk to the children's clinical psychologist before leaving at the end of the day. Felicity needed help beyond her scope.

Early that afternoon Sienna hung seven-year-old Andrew Dixon's file on the hook at the end of his bed and turned to his parents. 'Andrew's responded well to his surgery. His bloods are back to normal, indicating there's no more infection.' The burst appendix had temporarily knocked the boy for six. 'As for his appetite, it's coming on in leaps and bounds.'

'When can we take him home?' asked his exhausted father.

Sienna smiled. 'Tomorrow morning after I've checked to make sure everything's still going how it should.' She loved giving out the good news.

Andrew's mother was on the verge of tears. 'Thank you so much for everything you've done. I hate to think what would've happened if we hadn't got him here in time.'

'Don't torture yourself with that. You did get him here, and soon he'll be creating mayhem at home and you'll be trying to shush him up.'

'Thank goodness for the rescue helicopter. The pilot's great and the doctor awesome. He was so calm even when it was so serious.'

Sienna's heart leapt. 'Who was your doctor?'

'Harry someone. I'm going to write to the head of the rescue base saying how good he was.'

'That's always a nice thing to do.' Harry won

people over so easily, no doubt his charm and smile coming into play. He hadn't won her over. No, but she'd hadn't been able to stop thinking about him all week. Sienna studied these two in front of her. 'Andrew's going to sleep for a while. Why don't you take a break?' They'd sat at his bedside most of the past two days and nights. 'Go to a café and have a decent meal. Not a hospital one that's unrecognisable. I'll be here and the nurses will keep a close eye on your boy.'

'But what if he wakes and asks for us?'

'Your phone numbers are on file.' And the nurses were adept at calming upset children. 'Go on. Get out of here and have some couple time.'

'Couple time? What's that?'

Don't ask me.

'Remember you're about to return home to three boisterous kids,' Sienna said. She'd met Andrew's siblings yesterday, and the ward hadn't been quite the quiet haven it was supposed to be while they were here. 'Time to yourselves is what you both need.' Sienna all but shooed them out of the room.

Andrew's father nodded as he passed her.

'You're right. A short spell to ourselves will do wonders. We'll be at that café on the corner if anything changes.'

'It's not going to.' Sienna watched the couple walk away and for a moment wished there was someone special in her life to go have a meal and coffee with, to help her let go of all the hang-ups from a normal day on a children's ward. Someone like Harry? Definitely not. He was too sure of himself for her liking. So if she wasn't liking him, why this sensation of slipping on ice whenever she was near him? She'd seen first-hand how caring a doctor he was with Fliss, and that always scored points with her. He just wasn't such a caring neighbour. Was that a big deal? They might've got off on the wrong foot, and a simple conversation could correct that. Did she want to fix it? She was single for a reason, wasn't prepared to risk the hurt of being dumped again. Her life was contained, probably too contained, but it was comfortable. Safe. Boring?

'Go home, Sienna. Take time out for yourself.' Dale appeared in front of her, refocusing her errant brain.

'It's just gone two. I've got hours to go. Anyway, I told Andrew's parents I'd be here while they take a much needed break.'

'I've got it covered.' The head of Paediatrics was studying her as if he'd never seen her before. 'You've put in ridiculously long hours this week, as always.'

'That's how the job goes.'

'Most of us have a life outside these four walls that we actively try to participate in with family and friends, not spend our energy avoiding.'

But she didn't have family close by.

You do have friends in town.

Who were equally tied up with work as she was.

'Spread those wings, Si. Lighten up a bit.'

Yes, Dad.

'Take the whole weekend off. I've got your patients covered,' Dale remonstrated like a harassed parent. 'You're not doing yourself or anyone else any favours working all these ridiculous hours.'

I need to make sure I'm busy all the time.

But he was right. She had put in uncountable hours throughout the week, and even for her she was overtired. It was time to relax. And honestly, not to have to think about medications and results and children in pain sounded like bliss. It'd be a rare treat—if only she knew what to do with it. 'I'm out of here.'

Walking off the ward in the middle of the afternoon should've been exciting. Instead it was…worrying. Hours stretched ahead. Her father was right: she was far too ensconced in her life of all work and no play. But how to change? Where to start?

At home, standing on her narrow deck, Sienna couldn't come up with anything to do with this precious time out. It felt alien. The sun was still in the sky. The birds still tweeting. Had she really become so rigid in how she lived that she couldn't think outside the square?

Too serious, my girl. You need to relax sometimes.

Staring across her front lawn, Sienna noted the grass needed cutting. While the area was pocket-sized, the thought of hauling out the electric mower didn't excite her. Not that it ever did, but keeping the grass under control was one of those things she did to feel on top of her world. Pathetic.

Deliberately turning away, Sienna glanced across at the adjoining apartment. If Harry was at home she might be tempted to take a bottle of wine over and apologise for being such a grump last week. Her fingers tingled and she flexed them to relax the tension taking hold in her muscles. She did want more excitement outside of doctoring in her life, right? But with an attractive man who managed to get under her skin even when she was mad at him? Why not? Go for broke. Or go put her head under the pillow and not come out for a month. That should work.

Spinning around, she headed inside, away from that lawn, those shut windows, the car that needed a wash. In the lounge she automatically flicked a straight curtain straighter.

Stretch your wings.

Yeah, right. Like how? Picking up her phone, she checked for messages, pressed speed dial for her friend Anna. 'Hey, sorry I'm so late returning your call but it's been one of those days.'

Anna laughed. 'When isn't it with you?'

'Says the lawyer who never goes home before midnight. So what's up? Want to have a meal downtown tomorrow night?' Girlfriends united. Boring if fun. Why did she glance across to Harry's place? Nothing would ever happen between them.

'We can celebrate. As of this morning you legally own every last nail and tile in your swanky apartment.'

'I'd forgotten you were filing my petition today. So Bernie's finally paying up? After three years arguing? Unbelievable.' Sienna's heart stuttered. 'This is great news. I'll never have to think of him again.' The lying, cheating fiancé who'd decided he preferred to live with the woman he'd reconnected with at his school reunion than marry her when for years he'd sworn he loved her more than his high-end car and multi-million-dollar home.

'It's all wrapped up, plus there's a bonus. He's paying your legal costs and money for half that rental property you bought jointly.'

'My shout for tomorrow night. Cortado's.' Their favourite place for major celebrations. Putting the phone down, Sienna again checked the time, but only minutes had passed. 'Now what?'

Go for routine.

In Titirangi over an hour later she pinged the locks on her car, swung a leg over her cycle and headed up the winding road leading to Piha Beach. Almost immediately the high humidity had her in a sweat. Good for the muscles, not so great for her breathing, but she kept pedalling hard. This would get whatever was eating her out of the system. She was not thinking about Harry, right? Not picturing that good-looking face or the smile that increased the speed with which her blood moved through her veins. Not at all.

A car swerved around her, the passenger jeering about her butt as it passed.

'Get a life, will you?' she snarled between breaths. Why couldn't people leave others to get on with what they enjoyed? What was so much fun about being rude to strangers?

Cycling was her time to relax, because she concentrated entirely on riding and often forgot what had got her on the bike in the first place. Except today it wasn't working.

What did Harry do for relaxation? Apart from hold noisy parties for upset colleagues, or stay out overnight maybe? Did she really care? Unfortunately she might. Though she shouldn't. He was on a temporary contract and would soon be gone again. It had taken months for her to trust Bernie enough to get close to him, not weeks, so she could forget all about getting to know this man. Hard to do, that. He just seemed to pop up in her mind whenever there was a free moment.

The front wheel wobbled in thick gravel. So much for concentrating on riding. Shoving the neighbour and the world out of her mind, she focused on getting to the top of the busy road without taking a break.

Harry had muscles in all the right places and made whatever he wore look superb. Of course she'd noticed. It would be rude not to. Some sights weren't made to be ignored. Bet he did some form of sport or worked out. Was she so desperate for changes in her life she was hallucinating about the neighbour? Except Harry wasn't a fantasy and her reactions to his physique were all too real. Oh, yes, real and solid and tempting. Damn it. Next stop, the library for a pile of books to keep her entertained until this feeling passed. Probably about when Harry left town.

Wheel-wobble. Again. Her cycling had taken a turn for the worse.

Deep breath, focus, right pedal down, left up.

Left down, right up. That's it. Careful, sharp bend and steep decline. Squeeze the brake, change gear. Concentrate.

It worked. Until the road straightened and the incline lessened, giving her nothing to concentrate on so hard. Nothing except the man persisting in getting in her head space. What would he be like in bed? He exuded confidence in everything else that she'd seen so it followed that—

Toot-toot.

Sienna swerved abruptly, away from the centre of the road, and towards—over—the edge. Her front wheel dropped abruptly, alarmingly. Her body flipped forward, her hands gripping the now useless handlebars, her legs still pumping, even though she was in freefall; down, down, down. Bushes tore at her, twisted the cycle left then right, and on downward. The momentum compounded the speed. More bushes, bigger now, snagging at her, tearing across her face, her arms. Then she was upside down, slamming the ground with her shoulder, tossed sideways, with the cycle she still held on to with a fierceness she couldn't explain now twisted between her legs. Pain tore through her, then a thud.

Bounce. Bounce.

Slowing.

A tree blocked her path.

Thump.

Blackness engulfed her.

CHAPTER THREE

SIENNA BLINKED HER eyes open, gasped at the pain filling her body from every direction. 'What happened? Where am I?' There were dark clouds in her head, along with pulsing, banging symbols of pain. Dragging her eyelids up, she stared at the scene in front of her. Trees, bushes…

Darkness took over again.

'Hello?'

She was having a nightmare. Any second now she'd wake up and find herself on her bike heading down the hill towards the beach. Bike. Hill. Rolling over and over.

'Can you hear me?'

A groan escaped her constricted throat. She'd gone off the edge of the embankment, a sheer drop down to these bushes. The pain was really making itself known, as if her body had a grudge with her. In her legs and back, her arms, the left shoulder—sucking in a breath, she tried not to think about what that might mean. She needed to toughen up, check herself out instead of panicking. Work out what the damage was and make a plan for getting out of here.

Moving could be detrimental. Spinal damage is a real possibility.

'Are you all right down there?'

That persistent voice was annoying. 'Go away. I'm trying to think here.'

'I don't know if you can hear me but I've phoned for help.'

So the voice wasn't in her head. There really was someone up on the road. She wasn't alone. As she opened her mouth to holler a reply her lungs filled with air and her upper body moved. Pain splintered her and the blackness rolled in again.

Thwup, thwup, thwup.

The bushes flattened and the trees swayed. A helicopter filled the little view Sienna had of the sky when she next pulled her eyes open. A bright red-and-yellow rescue chopper. Gratitude swamped her. Whoever that man was who'd called for help, she owed him big time.

A figure attached to a thick rope was lowering in her direction. Help had arrived. In a pair of red overalls. She'd be out of here in no time. Then she'd be able to get patched up and back on her feet.

If my injuries aren't serious.

A shudder tripped through her, her tightening muscles sending warning signals of pain to her brain. It was tempting to move, to try to sit up, to prove she was all right. The doctor in her kicked in. *Stay still.* Let the rescue crew do their job. But waiting had become difficult. What if she'd broken her spine? She was a paediatrician. She didn't have time for learning to walk again, or never walking...

'Hello, this is becoming a habit.' A familiar, husky voice broke through her fear. 'Harrison Frost, your neighbour.'

Harrison. 'Not Harry, then.' Harrison was way sexier than Harry. Ah? Hello? Head injury talking? Sex while smashed up on the side of a hill? Why not? That'd certainly be creating a new norm for her. Don't forget, she told herself, that if she hadn't been thinking about him she wouldn't be lying here afraid to move.

'Good, you're cognitive. And yes, I go by Harry most of the time.' The guy was snapping open the hooks that held him to the rope and giving the thumbs-up to someone above in the chopper, at the same time speaking into a radio. 'Take it away.'

What were the odds he'd be the one coming to her rescue? But then, nothing seemed to be going right for her lately, so those were as short as the two-year-old with pneumonia she'd treated this week. She could only hope Harry was more forthcoming in his attitude as a doctor than as a neighbour. 'You didn't bring the music.' Anything to keep from the pain getting stronger with every breath.

'I would've if I'd known it was you who'd taken to flying off the side of roads.' Harrison shucked out of his backpack. 'Right, let's check you out. You haven't moved since coming to a stop against the tree?' He began disentangling the cycle from her legs.

'Of course not.' Unless she'd moved while out cold. 'I need a neck brace first. My left shoulder is possibly broken. My right ankle is giving me grief, but as for internal injuries I'm certain I'm in the clear.' The pain throbbed up and down both legs. Bruising from the bike when she'd landed?

'Leave those decisions to me. Obviously

nothing wrong with your head. You're stringing sentences together and enunciating clearly.'

'I am a doctor.' And it was his fault she'd ended up in this mess, tramping through her mind the way he had.

A small smile lifted one corner of his mouth. 'Right now I'm the doctor, you're the patient, and I get to make the diagnoses, starting with doing the ABCs.'

Her airway was fine, the proof in her relatively easy breathing when pain wasn't interfering. 'Might have known you'd be bossy.'

His smile hit her hard. 'It goes with the territory and stroppy patients.'

Putting as much indignation into her voice as she could muster, she growled, 'I'm stroppy?'

'Yep.' Harrison's eyes were focused on her chest, purely to check she was breathing normally.

A twinge of regret came and went. She didn't want him thinking of her as anything other than a patient. Not really. But it was nice to be noticed by a good-looking guy occasionally. 'Have you always worked on the helicopters?'

'No, I'm an emergency specialist so I've spent most of my time in emergency departments.

Working on rescue choppers is different. It takes some getting used to not having a whole department filled with every bit of equipment I require.' He might be talking trivia but there was nothing trivial about the way he was checking her over.

She could get to like this man. If she didn't already.

'I can imagine.' He was right. She had to let go and trust him to look after her, but it was hard. She never gave control to anybody over even the most insignificant thing. And this wasn't insignificant. Thump, thump, went her head. Her mouth opened but she couldn't give him the go-ahead. She just couldn't.

As he carefully removed her helmet, Harry asked, 'Have you lost consciousness at any time?' Seemed he had no difficulty taking charge, regardless of what she thought.

As he's meant to.

'Twice. I think. Maybe three times.' And about to again if the clouds gathering in her skull were any indication. She'd been trying too hard to say what was needed without slurring or forgetting what she had to tell him and it was taking its toll.

'Pulse is rapid. I'd say you're in shock.' Firm yet gentle fingers touched her neck, her skull, her jawline. If only they could stop the pain.

She guessed she couldn't have everything.

Please let me be able to walk away from this.

Fog expanded in her head, pressing at her skull.

'Sienna, can you hear me?' Was that Harry? Harrison. 'Yes.' But there were drums in the background. The humming in her ears also added to the noise.

Firm fingers slid over her skull, pressing lightly, feeling for trauma. 'From the state of that helmet you hit something with your head. At least the helmet did what it was meant to. There doesn't appear to be any damage to your skull, though you probably have mild concussion.' Then he was listening to his radio, and confirmed what she heard loud and clear. 'The weather's closing in. The guys above say we have to hurry or we'll be stuck here until the storm passes.'

'What storm?' Come to think of it, she was feeling chilly. But that would be shock. Wouldn't it?

Come in, Dr Burch. You know your stuff.

'Am I cold or is the reaction to my crash setting in?'

'Both,' answered Harry, slipping a neck brace into position. 'This'll keep your head still.'

A male voice came through the radio in his shirt pocket. 'Sorry, have to back off now, Harry. Hang in there. I'll return as soon as viable.'

The tree she'd come to a halt against rustled and leaves dropped onto her. 'Don't let them go.' She had to get to hospital and sort out her injuries.

'Not a lot of choice,' Harry told her before easing her cycling shoes off. 'Can you feel me touching your toes?'

'Yes.' Relief swarmed through her.

'Wriggle them.' There was a reciprocating relief in his dark eyes. 'Good.'

Neck immobilised, tick. Feeling in feet, double tick. 'My shoulder?'

But Dr Harry was working his way up her legs, as in how a doctor would, not a lover. As she'd said earlier, this just wasn't her day. 'Your ankle's okay. Lots of bruising would be about as bad as it gets.'

Those fingers... Sienna sighed. Gentle, and

warm, and enticing. As if she could succumb to their hidden promise.

Where did that come from?

Had to be the bang on her head. Her brain had been derailed. Whatever, it was good to let these wonderful sensations take over. They relaxed her, made her forget a little of why she was here, and had her thinking one bottle of wine wouldn't be enough to take across to his apartment.

Dr Deep Voice continued. 'Unfortunately I didn't bring my X-ray machine to check your shoulder.'

Typical relax-the-patient talk. 'Funny…not.'

'For someone who's knocked herself out, bashed up her body and got into difficult terrain, you have a lot to say. But I can tell you the shoulder's not dislocated, and from the normal angle I'd hazard a guess it's not broken either.'

'I'll give that box a half-tick, then.'

Large, oh, so gentle hands prodded her stomach, moved up towards her ribcage. Deep concentration tightened his face.

'Ow!' She gasped as sharp pain struck. 'What—?'

'Take it easy.' He pressed her back against

the ground with that firm hand she was beginning to recognise for its warmth and strength.

Sienna hadn't realised she'd moved. 'Tell me.'

But he'd turned away to talk into the radio that had crackled into life against his expansive chest. 'Yo… What's happening up there?'

'Weather bomb coming in fast. You're going to have to hang in on your own for a period yet. We'll be back ASAP.'

She mightn't know the voice but she sure knew that warning. ASAP meant 'in a while, even a long while'. 'Isn't there another way out of here?' There was a road just above them.

Harry was shaking his head. 'Afraid not. You picked about the worst spot on this road to fall off. The slope is all but vertical. Hauling you up it is not an option. We're going to have to wait it out. The thermal blanket will protect you from the wind and keep you warm.'

The wind had picked up, and now rain slashed at them, driving in sideways. Sienna shivered. Every part of her body hurt, some worse than others. She wanted to cry from it all but instead drew a deep breath and held on—just. Things kept going from bad to worse, and she only had herself to blame. 'But if there aren't any broken bones or internal injuries I can give getting to the top a crack. Better than lying here.'

'You banged your head, remember?' He was removing nasal prongs from a container. 'Do you remember what happened?'

'I—' lost focus and rode into the middle of the road then executed an abrupt dodging movement when a car came up behind her '—made a mistake.'

Thinking about my job. About you.

Really? She'd been thinking about Harry while riding? Yes. She had. Which went to show how easily she could be distracted. 'Are you giving me oxygen?' Of course he was.

'Your breathing's a little rapid. Best we get that settled.'

'Got an electric blanket in that pack?' Shivers were taking over.

'Sure have.' He locked that dark gaze on her. 'Relax. We'll get you out of here, and in the meantime I've got you. Don't worry about a thing.'

Had she been that transparent? Worry about her injuries despite his optimistic assessment was building like a volcano about to erupt. This could've been a disaster, might've been the end of everything, and she was afraid of tempting fate by accepting she hadn't been seriously injured before the hospital gave her the all-clear. With effort she hunted for something to talk about that might keep those concerns a little quieter. 'You're Australian.'

'Well spotted.'

'Where from?' Hard to concentrate when her mind was trying to shut down, but the longer she stayed awake the more she might learn about this man. Because despite—or was it because of?—being stuck on the side of a hill going nowhere in a hurry, she wanted to learn more about him, to make up for the weeks they'd been neighbours and strangers.

'Melbourne.' He wasn't making it easy.

'City or beyond?'

'City. The swanky part of town. Boys' college, box seats at the MCG, and all the rest of it.' A lime would be sweeter than that tone.

'Why Auckland now?'

Answer fast before I fall asleep.

'It's where the next job came up.'

That woke her a little. 'You move around a lot?'

Like my dad does?

'Depends on what turns up.'

If she could move she'd shake him, but then she'd already known how irritating he could be. Worse, he was sounding more like her father with everything he said. 'You ever just talk for the sake of it?'

To keep your patient distracted from her situation?

'I have been known to.'

She gave up. That darkness was pressing in, relieving her of any control. *Don't think about that.* Sienna groaned and slurred out a question that was totally irrelevant to anything. 'What time is it?'

'Five thirty.'

Harry continued tucking the thermal blanket around Sienna, all the while keeping an eye on her. It wasn't hard. Even injured and stranded out in the middle of a storm she was beautiful, and stirred his blood relentlessly. Once they got out of this mess he was going to have to do something about Dr Frosty, who wasn't as frosty as he'd first presumed.

She used it to cover real emotions. Emotions

he'd noticed flitting across those stunning blue eyes during the time they'd been together on the hill. He'd seen how her decline into sleep had briefly halted when he'd answered her question about moving around a lot in the affirmative. Had someone important kept moving away from her when she needed them? A partner; husband; lover? He could keep guessing or get on with being the emergency doctor he revelled in being. 'Have you got an underlying condition I should know about?' he asked without any hope of getting an answer. The shock had caught up and she was that far gone now.

But, 'N-no-o.' Sleep slurred her speech.

He could relax on that one. 'Good. You're safe at the moment. Our pilot's one of the best and he'll return the first instant he can. We'll get you out of here in one piece, Sienna.' But only when it was safe to do so. Another helicopter crash was not on the cards.

'Safe?'

He nodded. As if she saw that. 'Very safe.'

Her eyes opened, surprise momentarily replacing the other emotions swimming there. 'Am I really—?' She swallowed, tried again in that slurred whisper. 'In one piece? You weren't feeding me the happy-clappy line to keep me calm until we're away from here?'

'I wouldn't insult you. Nor would I feed you expectations that could be stomped on once you're in hospital. You have mostly bruises,' he repeated his earlier diagnosis to shore up her failing confidence. 'Lots of them. I still don't think there's anything to worry about regarding your shoulder except severe bruising. Possibly some rib damage, but I'd say you've come off lightly.' When her eyes widened with hope, he rushed in. 'Not lightly enough that I'm about to haul you up the bank with a rope around your waist. We're still at the bottom of a precipice with a summer storm rampaging around our ears.' Was that hail? It wouldn't surprise him, given the ferocity of the wind and rain pounding them. Thunder backed him up; no lightning flashes but then the clouds delivering the icy pellets were hiding that. Auckland was known for its short, sharp seasonal storms. In this case, not what the doctor ordered, but then when did anything ever go completely right on a job? It was the nature of the urgent scenarios to throw spanners in the works. Big ones mostly. And often through weather.

Digging into the pack, his fingers closed around a concertinaed umbrella which he pulled out and opened to hold above his patient, shielding her from the worst, angling it so a gust of wind didn't turn it inside out. It would be best if Sienna slipped into unconsciousness again so she didn't feel discomfort and had no idea of the time ticking by as they waited for the chopper to return. He could only hope it was today. The weather reports had forecast more storms over the next twelve hours at least.

Beside him Sienna moved. Trying to roll over? Harry placed his free hand on her good shoulder. 'Easy. Don't move.' Their ledge wasn't as wide as he'd like. Sienna had been extremely lucky that that tree had halted her tumble.

'Mmm...umm...'

So she *was* out of it, unaware of where she was, and more importantly getting a break from the pain. Good. He tied the umbrella to the base of the tree so it sheltered her face before taking running checks again. Concussion seemed to be her most worrisome injury, and he could handle that. Relief that she hadn't fractured any major bones or suffered serious internal injuries spread through him, though from her reaction when he'd touched her ribcage it was possible she'd cracked one or two ribs, or torn cartilage from the bones. But she'd be able to lift a glass of wine when he took that bottle next door. Because he was going to. Without a doubt. It might be tempting a snub, but he'd risk it. Thanks to this accident they were inextricably linked, and he'd use that to his advantage. He wanted time with her that much. And after today she couldn't deny he existed.

On his haunches, hunched under the edge of the umbrella, Harrison studied the captivating face he'd first admired a week ago. Shock and pain had dimmed her raw beauty, but there was no denying the fine features and that classic facial structure sucking him in. 'So we're both doctors.' Was that attraction stirring his groin? No. Too weird, that idea. This was purely because Doc Not-So-Frosty had a figure that demanded attention from all working parts of a man's body, and a face to take the edge off anything she might say.

Again Sienna moved. Again he held her still. 'Shh, easy does it.' He kept his voice low and soft, sleep her best option for now. When she didn't relax he sat next to her, stretching his legs the length of her body so they were touching side by side, and began soothing her hand, making light circles with his fingers. Slowly, slowly, the tension fell away from her muscles and she stopped moving her hands and feet. Had she been unconsciously checking again to see that she hadn't damaged her spine? It had been her biggest fear when he'd arrived, and who could blame her? Cycling accidents were notorious for shoulder injuries, but spinal damage was up there too.

His radio barked into life. 'Harry, are you receiving? This is Ginger.'

Their pilot. 'Harry receiving loud and not so clear. What's up?'

'You're stuck there for a while yet, I'd say. What's the situation with your patient?'

'GCS four.' Not bad considering how rapid her descent must've been, and the bone-jarring—if not breaking—halt against the tree. But the score could change rapidly, dropping to a dangerous level if Sienna got too cold or there was internal bleeding going on he hadn't discovered. But all indicators said she was lucky there. He turned his back on her, just in case she wasn't as out of it as he believed. 'Don't let that fool you. I want her out of here ASAP. Her temperature has taken a dive since the hail came across.'

'Roger. Understood. I'm talking to the weather gods every few minutes but so far they're ignoring me.'

'Keep at it.'

'I'll get back to you in thirty unless the all-clear comes through. Hang in there and keep her safe, man.'

As if he'd do anything else. Keeping safe came first, especially for his patients. Not so much for himself. He'd always been a bit of a risk-taker, snowboarding off mountain ranges and deep-water diving in shark-infested waters; though with that one there'd been a team of experts at his back. Not that his parents would've noticed if things went pear-shaped. His brothers understood his apparent recklessness, though they didn't condone it, but to their credit they left him to his own decisions, something he appreciated almost more than anything. They weren't meant to feel guilty for him copping all the blame their mother had dished out for disasters big and small when they were young—and not so young. He was the cause of her disappointment with how life had served her, so his brothers had been spared the vitriol. Because they'd been wanted, planned for. Unlike him.

Harry swallowed the familiar bile. These days, since his mother had taken over control of the multinational company his grandfather had created, the family was more divided than ever. He and his brothers were together in their need to get on and make lives for themselves, while their parents fought endless battles between themselves over who was in charge of the company. His siblings had found love with wonderful women and dived right into their own families, putting distance between themselves and the parents who might've wanted them but didn't show much affection towards them. Finding a woman to love and have a family with was not something Harry planned on doing. His one and only serious relationship years ago had turned out to be as nasty as his parents' one, and confirmed his belief he did not want that for the rest of his days. Just as he didn't want to be told to try harder, become greater, aim higher. If someone couldn't love him for who he was then he wouldn't bother.

He'd learned to be happy with his single status; he just wasn't always so careful with himself.

He reached for Sienna's wrist. What was her pulse now? Her wrist was slight and her skin satiny. If anyone around here had a high pulse rate it was him.

'So you're a doctor, and a cyclist. What else interests you?' he asked into the wind-tossed space in an attempt to distract himself from the heat tripping up his arm from where his fingers still touched her skin. Lowering her arm, he pulled back. 'I know loud music isn't one of your favourites, Doc Frosty.'

He barked a harsh laugh. Doc Frosty and Dr Frost stuck together on a hillside.

Ever since the night she'd stormed up his drive he'd been aware of her. Or rather, of how often she wasn't at home. It made sense now he knew her profession. Putting in long hours came with the territory. Which was one reason he loved his work. There was no time for anything else other than light, short relationships with women and easy-going friendships.

Those odd moments of longing for something he couldn't explain that came in the middle of a night shift when there was nothing happening but waiting in the tedious dark for a call that he always hoped wouldn't end badly for the victims were to be ignored. The unsettling need for something, someone, had to be banished. He was his own person and, once free of his mother's blame game and his wife's endless demands to be someone he wasn't, he'd vowed he'd never let someone else dictate how he lived, or where, or why.

His brothers lived the lives of their choice, and encouraged him to do the same, though they weren't always keen when he leapt off mountains with nothing more than a board strapped to his feet for safety. They and their families were his support system, the people he loved most. There wasn't room for anyone else. He'd tried once. Never again.

His eyes tracked across Sienna's exhausted face. Yes, she cranked up his libido something wicked. No, she wasn't going to become important to him other than as a patient at this point in time. Yes, he wanted to learn more about what made her tick. No, he didn't have any intention of spending time with her.

No longer than it took to share a bottle of wine, at any rate.

CHAPTER FOUR

'HOW LONG HAVE we been waiting for your lot to return?' Sienna stared through the semi-dark at Harry. His rugged face was in shadow while the lantern he must've had in his pack gave an eerie glow to their surroundings. He was so close it wouldn't take any effort to touch him. What would his skin feel like under her fingertips? Warm? Exciting?

Then he blinked and sat up straighter before reaching for her wrist, his finger instantly on her pulse. 'A little over an hour. Not long, considering.'

Definitely warm…and exciting. 'Hmmm…'

'What does "hmmm" mean?'

That she liked the spiky sensations going on up her arm from where he held her. 'Thank goodness you got here before the weather packed in or who knows what shape I'd be in by now? First thing I'm going to do once back on my feet is buy a lottery ticket. Who knows? My luck might still be running.'

His gaze cruised over her in a not-so-doctor-ish manner when she said 'shape'. A manner she could get to enjoy very quickly. His chuckle was delicious: more warmth, as well as comforting, and as if he was *with* her. 'I'll drive you to the shop when we're off the hill and the ED guys have tidied you up.'

Sienna shifted her numb butt and got stabbed with aches throughout her body for her effort. Her head pounded but thankfully her vision was clear. All the better to observe this annoyingly interesting man. Sticking her tongue firmly in her cheek, she asked, 'You hanging around Auckland for a day or two more, then?'

'Up until Christmas.'

'Then where are you going?'

'I'm starting to doubt you've got concussion. Your recall is superb. Remind me never to tell you anything important.'

A smile accompanied his words so she remained relaxed. 'As we hardly ever speak that's not likely to happen.'

Harrison grunted. 'Here's the thing. We seem to keep getting thrown together so I'm figuring we might as well get to know each other a little. Only as neighbours,' he added quickly.

'Sounds like a plan as soon as I'm mobile again.' Fingers crossed that'd be tomorrow, not months down the track due to serious damage.

'We can share a bottle of wine on the deck.'

So he was okay with the wine idea. She must've talked in her sleep. They couldn't have been having similar thoughts about getting together for a drink. Could they? How soon could he visit?

Downplay this.

She hadn't said anything in her sleep about how he made her blood sing, had she? Better concentrate on staying wide awake from now on.

He went quiet, and the haze in Sienna's head began to rule despite her worry about what she might say next. But the fog didn't take over as it had earlier. Had she run out of puff? Or was it that she was awake enough that images of her neighbour were rolling in? Leading her into temptation? As if. Stuck out here was so not the place for anything other than waiting to be lifted off.

Harrison sat beside her, his long legs stretched

out, his hands relaxed on his thighs. Hard to ignore. He was more than attractive. There was something dependable about him that activated all her buttons when she stopped thinking how exasperating he could be. The pounding started up again in her skull. Not Harrison's fault. Not even thoughts about him were to blame. She was falling asleep.

Falling. Over and over.

Sienna awoke with a jerk, and groaned.

'Hey, easy.' That hand she was getting inordinately fond of touched her good shoulder.

Something niggled from her dream. 'What if no one had seen me go off the edge of the road?'

'Let's not go there. You were seen and here I am.'

She could have broken her back, been left for days till someone found her, or worse.

'You need to relax, my girl. Spread your wings and fly.'

Sienna's eyes flew open. Her father was right. She had been missing out on so much. What if she had broken her back? That would finish everything. This had been a wake-up call she needed to heed. 'Bring that wine over the first time we're both at home.' Then she'd return the favour a few days later. If they got on well enough to repeat the date. Date? Not likely. Calling that a date only underlined how sad her life had become. Whether or not they had anything else to do with each other afterwards, spending an hour with Harrison meant she'd be making a start on getting out there to do things she'd only ever thought about. How was this for another? 'I'm going to sign up for flying lessons.' Plummeting down a hillside had a lot to answer for. But if that had gone horribly wrong there wouldn't be any crazy ideas to put into action.

'You want to become a private pilot?' Bafflement darkened Harry's voice. Then he reached for her wrist again. Did he think she was slipping into gaga land because of that knock on her head? He could be right, but she didn't think so.

That tingling thing on her skin was going on under his fingers. 'My father keeps telling me to spread my wings and try different things. I'm interpreting him literally.' Then she shuddered. 'Only problem is I'm a bit afraid of heights.' Though flying on a commercial flight had never caused any problems. 'So this could be a bit of a challenge.'

Respect blinked out at her. 'You need to do a bungee-jump from the Sky Tower. That'll cure you.' He laid her arm down against her side. 'All normal.'

'Glad you weren't taking my pulse when you made that crazy suggestion.' To be honest, she was surprised it had been normal when all the nerve endings in her wrist had been on high alert to his touch. 'You ever done a jump?'

'I get my thrills regularly dropping out of helicopters, so no need.'

'That's feet first on a winch, not upside down on a rope.' Could she do it? Yes, she could. If she didn't she'd crawl back into her safe box, probably never to come out again. She'd survived today's crash; the momentum needed to be carried on. 'Do it with me,' she challenged before she could put her brain into gear.

His eyes widened and those full lips tipped into a tummy-twisting smile. 'You're on.' He held his hand up, palm out towards her. 'It's a deal.'

Did he have to look so shocked at what he'd agreed to? There was no getting out of this one. She wasn't sure whether to be pleased, or downright terrified. Only time would tell. Raising her arm and biting down on the stabs of pain from wrist to shoulder, she lightly hand-tapped him back, and tried not to think about that large hand making hers look tiny and feel…? Just feel. It had been too long since the last foray into men and sex, and not once had she known this sense of the ground slipping out from under her. More likely that came from her precarious position perched on a steep hill-side. 'You didn't agree just to keep your patient happy?' She'd be gutted if he said yes.

'I never promise what I don't intend seeing through.' Harry's radio crackled into life. 'Yo, how's things looking?'

'We're coming in to get you. Ten minutes out,' was the reply.

Sienna sighed. Back to reality, and a challenge she'd initiated. Seemed if she was going out with a bang it was with someone sexy and good-looking and intriguing. And if she felt things were getting out of control too fast, Harry would be leaving in the not too distant future, so she wouldn't have time to make a dreadful mistake about getting too close to him. It took months for that to happen with her. Not weeks. Or days.

'You hear that?' Harry asked, already packing the kit.

'We're going home.' On some days hospital was as much home to her as her apartment, probably more. The only difference tonight being that she'd get to use a bed. Hopefully briefly.

'You'll be lifted up first. Do exactly what Connor says and you'll be fine.'

'That come with a guarantee?' Now was the time to find out how scared of heights she was. For one, she'd be totally reliant on other people, and she didn't do that very well. Hello? Bungee-jumping would be the same. She *was* going to be all right.

'Written? Or will you take my word for it?' Harry asked as he attached the harness that'd take her away.

'Get me out of here,' she smiled. At least she tried, but it was feeble. Now that the hill was about to be left behind she should be letting go of some of the restraints keeping her tense, but it didn't come naturally. She hadn't been in real danger of falling further, but she'd had no control over what happened to her. Still didn't, but she was headed to an environment she understood more than just about anything else. Time to find out every last detail about her injuries.

Then she was spinning in slow circles as the ground dropped away. A gasp escaped. That tree that mashed her helmet had saved her life. Beyond the pine was—nothing. A large, open space that didn't stop for metres, and then at a rocky outcrop. A shudder tore through her, another gasp drew air into her already full lungs. Definitely learning to fly. Or getting a pet cow or…

'Hello, Sienna. I'm Connor.' Already he was swinging her inside the helicopter. The clips keeping her harness and the rope joined were undone and dropped downward again, and she was lying on a stretcher, with tiredness seeping into every muscle, in her head, her mind.

Harry had barely clambered inside when Sienna felt the sway of the chopper as the pilot took them away from the hill.

'Last stretch.' Harry gave her a heart-warming smile. 'Soon you'll be back in control.'

He got that? This man was too good to be

true. Or too risky. She didn't want anyone being able to read her so easily, or so accurately.

Harry leaned closer. 'I didn't ask. How did you get out to Titirangi to go cycling?'

See? She really wasn't up to speed. 'I drove out. Did we bring the bag from my bike with us?'

Relief nudged her when Harry nodded. 'We did.'

'Thank you.' She owed him. 'Maybe I should be the one bringing the wine.'

'Your keys in this?' He held up the small bag that had been around her waist when she'd gone flying over the edge.

Her turn to nod. 'And phone.'

'I'll sort something to retrieve your vehicle tomorrow.'

'You don't have to do that.'

'You're right, I don't. But I will.'

She had no energy to argue. Nor any better ideas. She could ask Anna, but she'd said something about finalising a case for Monday. 'If you take me I can drive it home. What about my bike? Is it worth trying to get that back?' It had cost a small fortune.

'And risk falling down the hill again? I don't think so. Best talk to your insurance broker.'

There was that. The pitch of the rotors changed. 'We're at the hospital already?'

'Yes. Let's get you inside to the warmth.' Harrison began preparing to disembark her. 'By the way, you won't be driving your vehicle tomorrow. If nothing else you'll be stiff and horribly sore.'

'That's for me to decide.' But he was right. Driving was out for a day or so.

'We'll talk about it later.'

She wouldn't be seeing him later, not even in ten minutes' time. Thank goodness. He had a habit of pushing her too far when he wasn't happy with what she said. Once she'd been offloaded he'd be back in the air, heading to base and signing off his shift, which actually finished at least an hour ago by her estimate, and she could arrange things re the SUV to suit herself.

An annoying grin came her way. 'Lost for words? I don't believe it.'

'Get me out of here.'

Within minutes she was being wheeled into the emergency department by one of the nurses and—Harrison. Seriously? The guy had a cheek. He'd told the crew to head back to base without him, that he'd sign off on line. He was chatting non-stop to the nurse, of the female variety, and reporting Sienna's obs and injuries, or lack thereof.

She'd be lucky to get any proper attention. The nurse was all but panting as she listened to every word he uttered.

Remind me not to let my mouth hang open next time I'm thinking Harrison is hot. It's so unbecoming. Not to mention embarrassing.

'That's it,' Harry wrapped up and handed the star-struck woman the notes he'd filled out throughout their time on the hill. 'Who's on tonight?'

'Amy Roberts and Josh Barrett, and there are two house surgeons. One of those two will attend Dr Burch.'

'I'll see about that,' retorted Harry as he took over pushing her bed into a cubicle.

A thrill of amusement made Sienna's eyes widen.

Don't open your mouth.

She wasn't the only one Harry annoyed just by being himself. This man who alternated between irritating and distracting was going to get her the best care available. Or he was going to try. She couldn't remember the last time anyone had looked out for her in this way. Her father had used to when she was a child, and Mum, even Bernie had in the beginning, but since the demise of her engagement there'd been no one covering her back. Probably her own fault, since she'd been so intent in standing tall and in control, to save getting walked all over once more. This felt...?

Good. Lovely.

Oh, give over.

It was exciting. Until she wriggled her legs to get comfortable and the throbbing that had been going on in her calves upped the tempo and the pain, reminding her there were more important issues at stake right now.

A large hand landed lightly on her arm. 'Take it easy. You're not ready to go dancing yet.'

'I wish.'

Don't take your hand away. It turns me to jelly, sure, but suddenly I'm not minding.

And the look of disappointment on the nurse's face was priceless. For once Sienna liked the sensation of coming first with a man, even if only for few minutes. By the time the doctors had poked and prodded her she'd be wishing to be alone with her aching body, and hopefully going to sleep. By then Harrison would be kilometres away, probably getting ready for a night on the town.

'You like dancing?'

She couldn't remember the last time she'd let loose on a dance floor. Looking up at him, she admitted, 'I used to.' She'd been nimble on the floor, had an ingrained sense of timing, and always lost herself in the music. Put dancing on the list. Suddenly the reason she was in the emergency department on a bed struck her, and she turned her face sideways into the pillow. Her spine was in working order, there didn't seem to be any serious internal pain anywhere, just around her ribs, her skull wasn't mushed, but what if they were wrong? What if—?

'Stop it.'

Her eyes blinked open.

'You're not doing yourself any favours concocting all sorts of scenarios where you can no longer cycle, work, or dance.'

'Damned know-it-all, aren't you?' Sienna

snapped, but some of the knots growing in her belly backed off. Some of them.

Harry strolled into the general ward of Auckland Central Hospital at ten the next morning. Why he was going to visit Sienna was beyond comprehension. So much for thinking he knew himself well. Getting the keys to her SUV which he'd forgotten last night wasn't the main reason for being here, more of an excuse to see her. 'Morning, Sienna.' Damn, but there was little colour in those soft cheeks, and the sparkle hadn't returned to her eyes, the vivid blue now an overcast sky shade. He would not acknowledge the tightening in his chest, nor the urge to pick her up and hold her close until she smiled properly.

'Harrison. What are you doing here?' Flat-mouthed didn't suit her, even if he was more used to seeing that than the smile which tightened him in places best not remembered at the moment.

'Come to take you dancing.' One corner of that wide mouth lifted enough to know he'd hit the mark. 'Or we could book that jump off the Sky Tower for after lunch.'

'I won't be eating for hours before I go leaping off any building,' came her retort. And yes, a half-smile now.

Unbelievable how good that made him feel. How scared, too. 'So you've had a gourmet breakfast care of the hospital kitchen?'

'Something unrecognisable.'

'Any doctors been to see you this morning?' Highly unlikely, it being Saturday, but then everyone had fallen over backwards to attend to her last night. Seemed she was a very popular paediatrician. No serious injuries had turned up but Amy Roberts still insisted Sienna stay in overnight so they could keep an eye on her mild concussion.

'Amy just left. I'm allowed to go home whenever I'm ready.'

Phew. No ongoing problems from that knock on the head, then. 'I came to collect the keys to your vehicle, so I can give you a lift before Connor and I go collect it if you like.' It hadn't taken any persuasion to get his off-sider to go with him. Someone else who thought Sienna was the bee's knees.

'You've got this all under control, haven't you?' The smile had disappeared.

What'd he done wrong now? 'I'm only helping you out.'

Sienna glanced up at him. 'I know. Thank you.' A sigh rippled across her lips, and tightened his gut. 'I'm not used to people stepping up for me.' Shock registered on her face, as though she'd admitted something huge.

'It's no big deal.' He didn't want her thinking he might keep popping over the fence to do things for her. 'How were you planning on getting home?' So much for not putting his hand up to help further.

'I phoned my friend and left a message, but she'll be at the market, then going for a run, so who knows when I'll hear from her?' Again Sienna glanced up at him. 'I guess that's a yes, please. Thank you, I'd like a ride home. If it's still on offer.'

'Unless you want to stay in your hospital gown, you're going to have to squeeze back into those tight leggings.' Could hurt a bit, what with all the bruises she'd collected. By the time they'd got her to the ED she'd been black and blue from head to toe.

Her chin shot forward and he'd swear her teeth were clenched tight. 'No problem.'

'Then let's get this done.'

'You can wait outside.' More jaw-tightening going on.

'You're going to need help.' And he was a doctor. He'd seen it all before. Yes, but he hadn't seen Sienna, and he'd spent a lot of time fantasising about her in the early hours of that morning.

'Not from you, thanks all the same.' She swung her legs over the side of the bed, grimacing as those bruised muscles did their job. 'You can go find me a nurse.'

His hand lifted of its own accord, took her elbow. 'Let's make this as easy as possible.'

'Sienna, what have you done to yourself? I couldn't believe it when I saw your text. Why didn't you call me last night?' A tornado in the form of a tiny woman dressed in sports shoes, shorts and top spun into the room. 'Are you all right?'

Harry immediately stepped between the newcomer and Sienna to prevent those widespread arms slamming around her. 'Careful.'

'Anna, I'm fine.'

The woman skidded to a stop, her hands dropping to her hips. 'You look anything but fine. A cycling accident? What happened? Did an irresponsible driver cause this? Want me to talk to the police for you?'

A genuine, full-blown smile appeared on Sienna's face, lighting up her eyes, softening her cheeks.

Harry's stomach dropped to his toes. *I want one of those.* No, he didn't. Or shouldn't. They were dangerous. He'd be pulled under, have to fight his way back to the surface. Might never make it.

Sienna was talking. 'Take your law hat off, Anna. The accident was all my fault.' So why did she look sideways to him for a moment? 'I phoned to ask you to give me a lift home.'

'Seriously, Si, are you okay? No broken bones or anything?'

'I was very lucky.' Again she glanced at him.

Her visitor's head shot up and he was being stared at. 'I'm Anna McIntosh. Of McIntosh, McIntosh and Brown.' She underscored her name. 'Who are you?' Like, don't fool with her friend or there'd be trouble.

'Anna, this is Harrison Frost, the doctor who came with the rescue helicopter.'

He presumed that was a law firm Anna had

mentioned, one that everyone should recognise, and, being new to town, he didn't. He put his hand out. 'Pleased to meet you, Anna. While I work for the Rescue Service, I'm also temporarily Sienna's neighbour,' he added for a bit of mischief, not wanting to be fobbed off as the medic and nothing else. But what else was he? Apart from a man who got tight in the groin every time he saw Sienna? And the guy who'd suggested taking a bottle of wine over to her place?

Anna's handshake was firm for someone so slight, her scrutiny of him just as telling. 'Just when did you get Sienna to hospital?'

If he could have avoided answering he would have, because this woman was putting two and two together and he didn't like the accurate answer. But Sienna was as capable of answering as him, so he told the truth. 'Seven forty-five last night.' Now the questions would really start. Like why was he here this morning, did he have a wife and kids somewhere, was his job permanent? He knew them all and this woman most certainly had Sienna's back, which had to be good. Unfortunately for him, he didn't have a résumé covering his dating habits and status in his back pocket, because he too had Sienna's back—he just mightn't be as comfortable with that as her friend was.

'Enough, Anna,' warned Sienna.

'To put your mind at ease, Sienna fell about sixty feet through scrub and came to a halt against a tree which saved her life. And because she wore a helmet she got mild concussion, no major brain trauma.' Harry paused. In his haste to stop those questions he was speaking out of turn by mentioning Sienna's injuries, but a quick look to Sienna showed she had no issue with that. In fact she gave him a nod, so he continued. 'Apart from the concussion she has major bruising and the ligaments on one side of her ribcage are torn. That's very painful and only taking it easy will help.'

Anna reached over and gave her friend a gentle hug. 'I'm so glad you didn't do any permanent damage, Si. You don't need any more trouble.'

He knew it. He'd seen worry in her eyes last night as she evaluated the injuries she might have got. But he'd also felt there was lots more going on behind that frosty look she did so well and which no longer cooled him at all.

The need to protect her rose higher, surprising in its intensity. He looked out for family and patients. Sienna didn't fit either category, no longer being a patient and never going to be anything remotely like family.

'Tell me about it.' Sienna looked around the room and back to her friend. 'My next consideration is, do I replace the bike or do I stop riding and play safe?'

'Thought we'd decided over dinner the other night you'd done with playing safe,' Anna answered.

So Sienna was a cautious woman. With her choice of sports, or was her heart overprotected as well? And why was he even wondering?

Sienna stared at Anna, confusion darkening her gaze briefly. 'No, you came up with that idea. I never agreed. Not totally.' Then she grinned. 'But you never take any notice of anything I say, so no surprise there. Since you're here, can you help me get dressed and then drop me off at home?'

A thoughtful look came over Anna's face and Harry found himself under a kind of scrutiny that had the power of a high-calibre X-ray. 'I'll help you get dressed, but I can't take you home, sorry. I've got something to do in the city and,' she waved a wrist encircled with a top-of-the-range watch, 'I'm going to be late. Since Harrison's your neighbour, he can give you a lift.'

'What have you got to do?' Sienna demanded in her annoyed voice.

So he wasn't the only recipient of that tone. Harry would've laughed if he wasn't getting edgy over Anna leaving her friend with him. Sure, he'd said he'd drive her home, but it was the scheming gleam in the lawyer's eyes that rattled him.

'See a dog about a bone,' Anna answered with a little smile.

'You don't have a dog,' Sienna snapped as it dawned on her she was being set up.

'Nor a bone,' the other woman laughed. 'Now, where are your clothes? Harry, can you leave us for a few minutes, please?'

He found himself out in the corridor without realising he'd moved. That was one powerful lady. Anyone on the other side of the bench when she was prosecuting stood little chance. Behind the closed door Sienna's voice had risen, only to be overridden by her friend's calmer one. Whatever Sienna wanted—he suspected a ride home with her friend and not him—it wasn't happening.

Harry's stomach sucked in, and his hands tightened. He had offered Sienna a lift, and meant it with every fibre in his body. To be told he had to do it rankled. But not as much as Sienna trying to avoid him. Now was when he should be running down to his four-wheel-drive and heading out of the city for the day.

Someone needs to keep an eye on Sienna for today at least. She's been discharged but even mild concussion can be uncomfortable for some time to come.

Sometimes being a doctor came with obligations. It was not possible to turn his back on anyone in need.

Sienna is not an obligation.

Then what the hell was she, apart from an annoying neighbour, a good patient, and an attractive woman who had him asking too many questions of himself about her? Was the petrol tank of his vehicle full? He could go to Taupo for the day. Stay the whole weekend even. He wasn't back on duty until Monday.

'I'm ready.' A soft but firm hand touched his arm.

Stepping back from that light but intoxicating touch, he growled, 'Let's go.'

'Anna means well.' Sienna was wobbling on her feet.

Putting his hand over hers to keep her there, and balanced, Harry said under his breath, 'Sounds like you believe that,' then louder, 'I'm sure she does.'

'We've been friends since university when she fell in love with one of the students in my class. Our friendship has lasted while her marriage didn't.'

Why was Sienna telling him this? It wasn't anything he needed to know. Unless she thought he was interested in Anna. 'Sorry to hear that.'

Have you ever been married? Got a brood of kids somewhere?

There hadn't been any sign of ankle-biters around her place, but she could be the career woman while the father took care of them— alone. 'You weren't attracted to anyone in her class?'

'No.' Tension rippled off her.

Best leave that line of conversation alone. 'Are you Auckland born and bred?'

'No.'

'Where are you from, then?' He'd go with ignoring the tension, try to lighten the mood that had overtaken her.

'New Zealand.'

Give me a break here.

'Right.' The lift doors slid open and he stood back to let Sienna in first.

'I was born in Whangarei, had my second birthday in Invercargill, my third in Christchurch, fifth in Pukekohe, ninth in Waihi. Went to high school in Napier, so that covered five more birthdays. University in Auckland.' There was no bitterness or joy in that statement. 'We lived in a house bus.'

She'd been on the move most of her childhood. What about other friends? A shudder rocked him.

There wouldn't have been any when she was young.

Nor things like sports teams to join and stay with year after year. 'You've stayed in Auckland ever since?'

'Oh, yes.' Sienna was staring at the floor, seeing something he could only guess at. 'Returning to the same place, the same things, every day, is important to me. Don't get me wrong.

Being on the road all those years was fun, and I have some wonderful memories, but I prefer the sense of belonging that I get from my own home.'

Even he with his diabolical mother couldn't imagine not having some place to call home growing up. Not that he had his own home as an adult, but that was his choice and one he could change any time he chose. 'Your parents stopped moving around for you to go to high school?'

'I demanded they did—said I'd run away otherwise.' She suddenly looked very small. 'Mum had home-schooled me up till then, but she couldn't teach me algebra and physics and all the subjects required if I was going to become a doctor.'

Obviously it'd hurt her to make that demand. Determination must've been her middle name, though, if she'd stood up to her parents so adamantly.

Go, you, Sienna.

Now he understood her question to him about being a wanderer. Not that it mattered. His lifestyle suited him because he didn't want to settle down, be held in one place to make someone else happy. Sienna was safe from him. Now he understood he wasn't in danger of falling for her wiles because no woman was going to put her foot down and demand where he stopped, where he lived, what he did. Sienna had done that with her parents, she knew it worked, she'd do it again for something she believed in. She was absolutely the wrong woman for him— if he'd been looking for one, which he wasn't. Where was the relief of knowing that? It should be shoving aside these silly niggles of interest in who she was behind that professional façade she wore too easily, making him let it go. But he couldn't. 'Where are your folks now?'

They'd reached his four-wheel drive. Harry pinged the locks and opened the door for Sienna, helped her up onto the seat, saw her swallowing when she knocked her ribs. He also swallowed. When he'd taken her elbow to help her up he'd been hoping to save her from added pain.

It wasn't until he was on the road heading towards their apartments that she told him, 'Mum's still in Napier, living in her own home. She has a friend, Bill, to share occasions with, but not her house, while Dad's travelling all over the South American continent,' she said, sadness thickening her words.

'Last night you said he'd told you to spread your wings. He doesn't understand your need to be settled in one place?'

'He understands all right, he just doesn't agree. Says I'm missing out on too much. To some extent that's true, but I'm also winning in other ways.' She leaned her head back and closed her eyes, her hands tight balls on her thighs. 'I'm getting to watch my trees grow.'

'You have to do what's right for you, not live according to someone else's ideas. Not even your father's.'

Very wise, Harry.

But it was what he did. Lived alone, worked wherever a job came up, didn't have a house to call home, though he did own a string of properties he rented out. Didn't do anything to abide by his mother's edicts.

'Yeah,' was Sienna's answer to that gem of wisdom.

CHAPTER FIVE

SIENNA STOOD BY her kitchen bench, waiting for the kettle to boil, and wiped up splashes of water on the counter, rinsed and dried the tea-spoon Harry had dropped in the sink when he'd made her a coffee earlier and placed it in the drawer, handle to the right. Now what?

There wasn't a part of her body that didn't ache, and downright hurt in some places. Especially the ribs, because she'd forget and put her arm out to reach for something, and ping, pain would stab her. Bed was the best place to be, but it felt alien in the middle of the day. Alien, and uncomfortable, and rendered her useless.

So here she was, wondering what to do with herself, apart from swallow some more pain-killers. The problem with those were they weren't soothing what really ailed her. The accident had rattled her more than it had any right to do. It was all very well deciding it had been the wake-up call she'd unconsciously been waiting for. Quite another to know what to do with it.

Write a list.

What would a list of things to occupy her when she wasn't being a doctor, over-zealous house-tidy-upper person, or cyclist achieve? Apart from frustration at learning how insular she'd made her life? Her bike was now scrap metal, leaving two of those options to fill in her time. Doctoring was out for a couple of days. Not a week as Amy Roberts had recommended. Two days of hanging out around here trying to come up with ideas she didn't have a clue about would test every shred of patience she had. She wasn't familiar with relaxing in a sit-and-read, or do-a-jigsaw-puzzle, or cook-a-fancy-meal kind of way. This was her haven in that it was *her* front door that opened into *her* home filled with *her* furniture, and outside were *her* trees, but as far as doing random fun activities here? It didn't happen.

Her head ached enough as it was without her having to think. The short sleep she'd had on top of her bed after Harry left to go fetch her car hadn't improved her mood.

He'd out and out ignored her when she said

she'd arrange for someone to get her SUV. At least she hadn't been stupid enough to say it could stay where it was until she was fit to drive. She did like having four wheels and all the windows intact. Titirangi was a good neighbourhood, but not all hooligans knew that.

Harrison. Her finger tapped her wrist. An enigma. Today he'd guided her not only to her door when they got back from the hospital, but had taken the key from her shaky fingers, unlocked the door and, hand on her elbow, walked her inside to the kitchen, where he'd pushed her gently onto a chair and proceeded to make coffee and toast. Who did he think he was? This was her territory. She got to decide who came through her front door, and what they did once inside.

Tell that to someone who believes you. You enjoyed every moment of it—couldn't find reasons to keep him at a distance.

True. All of it.

The moment he'd gone she'd tossed the toast down the garbage disposal and the coffee down the drain. The hospital breakfast was still firmly lodged somewhere between her mouth and her stomach and nothing was getting past. Or was that because of nerves about her neighbour? Harry had a cheek taking over as though he owned the place, but he'd also acted as a friend. Like Anna usually did, before she had a brain fade and decided Harrison Frost was the man to be seeing to her needs. Sienna had a clear idea what needs Anna was thinking about. It was *not* happening. Even if her skin tingled and her fingers warmed whenever he was near.

The kettle whistled, clicked off.

Sienna stared at it. What was she doing? Coffee was still the last thing she wanted. Reaching to put the mug back in the cupboard, she knocked against the shelf and gasped as pain tore through her ribs. The mug slid from her fingers and shattered on the tile floor. Sweat beaded on her forehead.

Great. Well done. It had been given to her by her mother on the day she graduated from high school. An English, fine china mug with blue daisies painted around it, it had once belonged to her Welsh grandmother. Sniff.

Toughen up. But she had precious little from her past to appreciate that wasn't in her head.

Write that list.

Start with finding a replacement mug.

The sun was streaming through the wide picture window in the lounge as Sienna hobbled towards the leather recliner chair, picking up pen and paper from the sideboard drawer on the way.

Buy Christmas presents for all the kids on the ward to take in on my first day back at work.

Really? She'd never done anything like that before, but now a frisson of excitement caught at her. Why not? The parcels would have to be generic as she didn't know each child personally, but kids were kids, and they'd enjoy getting a gift.

The leather was warm from the sun. The paper remained blank. Sienna grew drowsy. The events of yesterday were playing havoc with her mind and body.

Spread your wings.

Take flying lessons, she scrawled, and let the ennui flattening her take over.

Blink, refocus. Collect stamps. She shook her head and held her pen firmly away from the paper. Not her thing. Anyway, where did a person find stamps these days?

Buy a new bike. Learn to cook Italian food. Design pretty scrubs to wear on the ward.

This was silly. Who wrote lists of how to get on with their lives? Besides, she didn't want to alter her life too much. She liked knowing how each day would pan out. Like she'd seen yesterday's crash coming? That only went to show it was better to keep some form of control going on. She dropped the pen and pad on the carpet. Didn't lean down to align the pen with the edge of the pad.

Wow. Letting loose, Si.

No, just too tired and sore to move. Her eyelids drooped.

The sound of her SUV coming up the drive woke her. But Harrison didn't stop there. Oh, no; using her remote control, he opened the garage and drove in. No stopping the guy when he was on a mission.

A mission to help, Sienna.

True. But she wasn't used to someone wandering through her space as though they belonged there. Then he was coming right inside, calling softly, 'Sienna, it's Harry. How're you doing?'

'Fine. I'm in the lounge.' She wanted him

to come in? For the first time in years it felt a bit lonely in here, but Harry wasn't the fix she needed. He was a good neighbour, he might even be becoming a friend, but she couldn't rely on him to be around forever. He was like her father, always on the move, and she would never go back to that lifestyle, not for anybody.

'Your car's back. I'm going to drop Connor home. Anything you need while I'm in town?' He came into the lounge and the room instantly shrank around her, the air filled with something intangible yet vibrant.

Talk about making it harder to push him away. Friendly, easy-going. It wouldn't be difficult to forget she wasn't in need of anyone else in her life. 'No, thanks.'

'You get any sleep?' He stood in front of her, those mesmerising eyes scanning her in a professional capacity. 'You still look exhausted.'

She supposed he was thinking medicine and nothing else. Why would he? A man with his looks and body could have any woman he chose, not some mashed-up doctor with chips the size of rocks on both shoulders. 'I got some,' she growled. 'I'm fine.'

Stepping back, he sighed long and loud. 'I'm

sure you are. I'm going to the supermarket. If you think of anything I can get you flick me a text.' He reached down for the pen and note-pad. 'Here's my number.' A quick scrawl and he handed the pad over and left the room with-out a backward glance.

When she looked down the annoyance he usually managed to crank up arrived in full force.

Stop sweating the small stuff, had been added to her list. *Her* list. Not his to play with. Bet he always knew what he was doing. Again she asked herself: Who did Harrison Frost think he was, coming in here like he owned the place, telling her what to do?

Snatching up her pen, she scribbled another line, just to remind herself she was in charge here. Not Harrison.

Then the pen fell from suddenly lifeless fin-gers as she stared at the pad. Oh, no. Big mis-take her writing that previous left-field thought on her list. Now she was definitely on the back foot. Harry would be laughing so much he'd wet himself.

Find a man to have a fling with.

The words beamed off the page. She might as well have hung a sign at the front door. What had she been thinking? Stuck on Harrison, that was where her brain had been. The sooner she got back to work the better.

Swinging into his drive, Harry stared across at Sienna's apartment. All the curtains were wide open, so she hadn't gone back to bed when it was obvious she was dropping with exhaustion. Stubborn woman.

Find a man to have a fling with.

He hadn't been able to get the words out of his skull for one second. His body was sitting up, ready to play ball, if he was the man she was looking for. But he rubbed her up the wrong way too often for that to happen.

He grinned. He'd also be in trouble for adding to her list. Bring it on. Feisty was good, kept things interesting, and put the brakes on getting too friendly. The problem being the more he saw of her the more he wanted to find out what made her tick. He wanted to be that man on her list. But did she actually mean it? Compared to other women he'd known, Sienna had keeping to herself down to an art form. His grin faded. Come Christmas he'd be out of here. He hadn't decided where to spend Christmas yet. It depended on where the next job was and when he'd be required to start—if one came up. Right now there was a scarcity of vacancies, which was a pain in the backside. Never before had he had a problem finding his next position; sometimes he'd had two or more to choose from. If nothing came up he'd take a break and go on a short trip somewhere exciting. The fishing was supposed to be good on the Coromandel.

Out of his four-wheel drive, he rescued the groceries from the warm back seat and headed indoors, and couldn't stop himself taking another look over the fence on his way. No sign of Sienna.

Groceries unpacked and stored, Harry checked his phone. No messages. No jobs. He gazed around the apartment, identical to Sienna's if he didn't factor in his tee shirt on the table, shoes by the fridge and yesterday's breakfast dishes in the sink. There hadn't been a single thing out of place next door. Not a one. How did anyone live like that? He couldn't, not if his life depended on it. There wasn't any point to being über-tidy.

Right now he had time on his hands that had to be used somehow. Not something he was used to. The washing he'd put on before heading out to Titirangi needed hanging on the line. That'd fill all of five minutes.

The lawns. They were getting out of hand, grass halfway up his calves in some places. The electric mower wouldn't make enough noise to disturb Sienna if she was asleep. Her lawns could do with a tidy-up as well. Though the grass would barely reach his ankles, he'd observed how she liked to keep it immaculate. Might win some points along the way.

Joke, Harry, joke.

An hour later Harry switched the mower off, and immediately wished he hadn't.

Sienna was coming towards him in an odd slow, limping kind of way with fire in her eyes. 'You didn't need to do that. I am quite capable of mowing my own lawns.'

'Thank you, Harry, for doing that job. I really appreciate it,' he snapped back, warning his heart to stop feeling quite so sorry for her. Heart? Didn't he mean head? Absolutely.

She stumbled, righted herself quickly. 'Yes,

well, sorry. I mean, it was kind of you, but it's a bit of a mess.' She blushed.

Finally some colour in those cheeks he had to resist running a finger down. 'A mess?'

The red hue deepened, and the blue in her eyes glittered like that lake when the sun was going down over it. 'Um, it's just that I like to mow up and down in straight lines.'

And he'd started at the far corner and gone round and round until he reached the centre. He stared at this woman. What the hell difference did it make? The grass was cut, done for another week; two if they were lucky with the weather and the spring temps didn't encourage too much growth. 'Whatever,' he said in a churlish tone that he instantly regretted. He wasn't a child, didn't do spoilt. If she wasn't happy with him then she wasn't. Not his problem. 'I promise not to mow them again.'

She closed her eyes, drew a long breath before opening them to stare at him with something he thought might be embarrassment creeping into her face. 'I am ungrateful, aren't I? Thank you for doing the lawns. I deliberately went cycling yesterday so I didn't have to do them, and that's unheard of.'

His stance instantly softened. 'You'd have been better off now if you had got the mower out.'

'I'd still have gone for a ride, and I'd probably still have been distracted by...' Her voice petered out as shock overtook that embarrassment.

'By?'

'It doesn't matter.'

'I think it does if it was a big enough distraction to send you off the road.' She'd glanced at him twice when Anna had asked how the accident happened.

Those full, tempting lips clamped shut.

'What was it?' It couldn't be anything personal because they didn't have a history, not one that spanned even a week. He wouldn't count that night and the loud music. But he hadn't been able to forget her since then. Maybe he should be counting it. Ah ha. Was that it? 'You're still annoyed that I didn't instantly turn the music down that night?'

'Not at all.' Her eyes were fixed on something over his shoulder, giving nothing away. Because she *had* been thinking about him while pedalling up the road?

Yeah, right. Get a life, Harry. If that's the best you can come up with you need to get out of here.

'It must've been another shock for you when I turned up at your accident site, swinging down on a rope from the helicopter.' If she had been distracted by him while cycling that would've felt weird to her. He tried to recall what she'd said, the expression on her face, but only came up with her anxiety and pain. No, he'd got it all wrong. So why was she looking everywhere but at him?

'Believe me.' Her head lifted, her shoulders pulled back until pain must've struck and she let go again. 'My crash had nothing to do with you.' Her composure wasn't working. Colour streaked her cheeks, those eyes he was coming to enjoy watching were widening and blinking as if batting away the truth. 'But yes, I was surprised when I saw you unhooking from that rope.' Colour rose again in her cheeks and down her neck.

Laughter rolled up his throat and blistered the air between them. 'I bet you were. Your worst nightmare coming to save you.'

She swallowed. 'Your words, not mine. I was

relieved that it was someone I knew. Okay, I didn't—don't—know you, but we had met, and it helped. Nothing to do with the medical side of things, though you were excellent, by the way.' Now she wasn't shutting up and would she ever regret that.

Harry interrupted. 'I'm putting the mower away. Then I'll come take your pulse and check your breathing.' And if they were fast? Would that mean she wasn't improving, or she was reacting to his touch? In reality it was his pulse that needed slowing.

'Don't bother. I'm going back to bed.'

Bed. If ever there was a word with too many connotations. But Sienna didn't blink, blush or look as if she'd made a mistake. Back under control? He hoped not. 'No problem. Just assure me you've taken your meds and are feeling as well as can be expected.' He could dampen down the heat that began expanding through his groin the moment she'd come out to blast him for doing her lawns. If she disappeared inside. If he concentrated really hard. Hard. Wrong word.

'I'm doing everything I'm supposed to, thank

you, Dr Frost.' Turning her back on him, she hobbled back inside her apartment.

Harry couldn't help himself. She wound him up something terrible. 'I'll look in later to make sure you're okay and prepare a meal for us. Anything you don't like, Doc Frosty?'

'Harassment from neighbours,' she threw over her shoulder.

The laugh that shot up his throat and over his lips was sudden and real. Damn it. He liked this woman. Frosty, feisty, annoying. None of those attitudes had put him off—instead they had ramped up his interest so much it could become dangerous.

Time to start ringing around people he knew and try harder to find a job that would take him away from here at the end of this contract.

A couple of hours later his phone rattled off a tune just as he was about to head across to Sienna's with a meal of steak, fries and salad to share. The tension that had been building since he'd left her earlier disappeared the moment he saw the caller ID.

'Hi, Lance. What's up?'

'Much the same as last time we talked. I'd swear the kids are growing a centimetre a day.

Soon they'll be patting me on the head and asking if I've eaten my greens. What about you? Fallen out with those Kiwis yet?'

'Not through lack of trying.' Aussies and Kiwis loved to hate each other, but put a third party between them and they were always allies.

'This isn't because you've found someone of the opposite sex to keep your bed warm and other things on the go for longer than a day?'

'Not likely. No, I just like the country.' And his neighbour. But Sienna wouldn't budge from here. So? He wasn't asking her to. 'What's this about? You don't usually ring for a chat.'

Lance grumped, 'It's been a while since we shot the gap over a beer.'

'Eighteen months. Your wedding anniversary.' His mate had found his perfect match. They'd have no issues about not wanting the same things for themselves and their kids.

'One in a million, I know.'

The love in Lance's voice stilled Harry's heart, turned him a little green. What was that like, knowing someone put you first most of the time, cared what happened in your day? Didn't want to hold you responsible for everything the world threw up?

Lance's tone changed to serious. 'Have you got your next position lined up yet?'

'Funny you should ask. There's a bit of a drought at the moment. Not that I'm too bothered. Something always turns up somewhere.'

'I might be able to help.' Lance hesitated, then, 'It'd mean coming back to Melbourne.'

No surprise there. Lance was based in his home town. 'I can do that for a short stint.' He'd returned to Melbourne twice to fill in at emergency departments, staying with Lance and his family, while avoiding his parents except for an occasional meal on the South Bank.

'Yeah. I figured.'

Got it. Not for a few weeks. 'How long?'

'Melbourne General needs an ED head of department for at least twelve months.'

The city was right up there on his list of great places. It only had one fault. His parents lived there. But he needed a job, and twelve months was better than eight weeks here and three months someplace else. Huh? Since when? He liked moving around. Yes, but not all the time. It was becoming a bit of a drag living out of a pack. Not literally, but with the limited contents he found more and more he missed having personal possessions around him. None of his favourite books to indulge in, having to wear the same old clothes week in, week out, not even his squash racket for when he suddenly felt like banging around a court. When had this started? His gaze drifted in the direction of the adjacent apartment. Not in the last week, surely? Not since the advent of Doc Frosty? If that was the case then he needed out of here quick smart. 'Tell me more.'

He got a brief outline before Lance said, 'I'll email the details tomorrow. But what's your gut reaction?'

Did he want this job? A job with no end date? In Melbourne? He wouldn't be able to avoid his folks forever. They'd want more than dinners. Did that matter? His mother couldn't belittle him any more, couldn't blame him for the roof leaking or the company not doing so well. Instead she and Dad could go on handing out the blame to each other as they'd started doing the day he walked down the front path never to return. As for Celia, she was long gone, living the high life in Sydney with some other poor sod to boss around.

'You trying to think up reasons to say no?' Lance asked.

'Yes. And no. I need to read the conditions and think this through.' Not that Lance wouldn't make sure everything was good to go. It was just— Hell, he didn't know what was holding him back, especially when he needed to find another job soon. Yes, he did. Melbourne. His parents. Sienna. Huh? What did she have to do with any of this?

'I recognise stalling tactics when I hear them.' Lance didn't hold back. 'Thought you'd put all that behind you.'

'I have.'

'So what's the "but"?'

'None of yours.' But this was his mate on the other end of the call. The man who'd helped him set up a flat after he left home, who'd stood by him when his parents had a very public spat at his graduation. There wasn't much Lance didn't know about him. 'It's not the past that's a problem. It's the future.' There. He'd said it out loud. Now he waited for the roar of laughter.

It didn't come. 'At long last.'

'Don't go getting ideas of me settling down with a woman and kids and the picket fence.' He didn't like the taste of that. Too cloying. 'It's more about stopping moving all the time, finding one place to set up home. I can still take jobs in different locations, but having a place to call my own to return to is starting to appeal.' He could still remain single, unfettered.

'Melbourne won't be that place, will it?'

Again his gaze travelled the distance between apartments. 'No. Might be. Haven't got a clue. After a good night's sleep I'll probably have changed my mind again.'

This is all new to me, and takes some getting my head around.

His eyes were still fixed over the fence.

'Go have that sleep and let me know about the ED job.'

Harry stuffed the phone into his back pocket. That meal needed delivering before it got too cold to eat. Sienna should be up and about by now. Her sleeps were short, followed by aimless wandering around the apartment. Not so aimless that she hadn't been writing a note on what to do once she was properly back on her feet. A grin lifted his mouth, and his spirits.

Bet she was spitting tacks at him over that. His grin widened. Then there was that fling idea. Did he want to take up the challenge? Hell, yes. But would he? Watch this space, he mused.

'Hello? It's your pain-in-the-butt neighbour, bringing dinner,' he called softly from the doorway.

No reply. Placing the plates on the table, he contemplated the merits of going to check on her for all of two seconds. He was a doctor and had promised Amy Roberts he'd keep an eye on Sienna for a few days.

Stepping out of the kitchen, he hesitated. On the floor by the lounge wall was a screwed-up piece of paper. It would have been no big deal in anyone else's home, but here, where nothing was out of order, it stood out. Recognising the blue page, he picked it up, opened it. And roared with laughter.

'Tell Harrison to stick his head where the sun don't shine.'

So he'd got to her. For some reason that made him feel damned good. Sienna Burch had got under his skin, so it was only fair he'd returned the provocation. They could continue brushing each other up the wrong way for as long as he was here. Apparently rubbing sticks together produced sparks, followed by flames. Would they do the same with each other? Finding out was going to be fun. There was a fling on offer. Maybe not to him—yet—but he wouldn't be himself if he wasn't at least open to the idea.

It couldn't hurt. Come Christmas he'd pack his bag and leave. For Melbourne? His grin died. Was this what he wanted? To finally return home? No. But if he stayed here he ran the risk of getting too involved with Sienna. He wasn't ready for that—and never would be.

Shaking away those irritating thoughts, he headed down the hall to Sienna's bedroom.

'Sienna?'

She stared up at the apparition filling her doorway. From where she sat on the edge of her bed Harrison looked impossibly big. She rubbed at her eyes to remove the sleep grit and looked again. Still large, and gorgeous. 'Hello?'

'How're you doing?'

'Could be better,' she admitted, feeling a little overwhelmed with his presence and the way her body ached from all the bruises while also coming awake in places that had been dormant for so long. This man did the strangest things to her, no matter how hard she fought him.

'Never thought I'd hear you say that.' His smart-alec grin undermined her further.

'What are you doing here?' she snapped.

'Dropping in on the lady next door, seeing as how her heart's working. I can already guess her head's not so flash.'

'Nothing wrong with my head.'

Nothing you need to know about. As for my heart, that's strictly out of bounds.

'Good, then I'll take your pulse and BP reading before we have dinner. Together,' he added with a certain satisfaction.

'In case you haven't noticed, I haven't spent the past hour in my kitchen cooking up a storm.' But she might've if she'd known he was dropping in.

That grin only increased. 'Ahh, but *I* have.'

'Damn it, you cook as well?'

'As well as what?' Harry slid the BP cuff he'd brought with him around her arm, those long fingers warm where they touched her skin. 'Sienna?'

'Sienna what?' Had she said something? Oh. 'You're good at swinging down to rescue people, and even better at taking charge and bossing someone around when they're not up to speed.'

The cuff was in place and yet his hand remained on it, his fingers still touching her as he pumped the bulb with his other. 'You don't like me helping out?'

'Liking and needing are two different things.' Locking her eyes onto his, she saw the black lighten as if she'd made him happy, which sent her stomach into a tailspin. There was no air in the room. Making Harrison happy was not a good idea. He'd get the wrong idea and she'd never be rid of him. Now there was a plan. Put that on the list.

He appeared to have to drag his gaze away so he could focus on taking the BP reading. 'I think I can make you like what you need.'

Sienna gulped, stared around the room. Her bedroom. Harrison was in her bedroom, supposedly taking obs and yet he was also flirting with her. Inappropriate? If it was she wasn't about to tell him off. It had been so long since a man had paid her attention. Make that, since she'd allowed one to. 'You probably think you know what I need as well.'

Harrison read the BP result, let the air out of the cuff, and pulled it off. When his eyes met hers again he was smiling in a teasing kind of way. 'I read your list, remember?'

Far out. He didn't hold back any punches. Or was he teasing? 'So you want to go shopping for a tea mug with me?'

'If we're starting at the top of the page then I guess I'll have to. Or I could drive you to the mall and wait in the car while you find what you're after.'

She'd already found what she was after—for the fifth thing on her list, that was. 'I'm not up to wandering around a crowded mall just yet.' Not up to energetic sex either, but that one she was more than willing to try.

The cuff was being mangled in his hands. 'We can always come back to that one later. Flying's out too, so you're making your way down the page without doing anything.'

But soon she'd reach the one thing she could act on—now. No. Too soon. But what was she waiting for? Here was a hot man, in her bedroom, available as far as she knew, apparently open to suggestions, and she was stalling. She needed air, space to think. Thinking, that was what she always did. Overthought things until the fun had gone out of them. Sienna shot to her feet. 'I don't…' The room spun. Strong hands caught her shoulders, held her steady. Everything around her was moving in circles. Everything except Harry. He was rock-solid, reliable, dangerous, exciting. Go for it. Lifting her head, she found Harrison watching her with resignation flattening that smile and darkening his eyes again.

'When you're ready, sit down again so I can take your pulse. Then we'll have dinner.'

Reluctantly Sienna withdrew from his hold and stepped around him to leave the room. The moment was gone. They were back to Harry helping her out as a neighbour who'd had an accident, not as a woman he might want to bed. 'My pulse is fine.' He was not going to find out it was off the wall. 'It's my stomach that needs attention now.'

CHAPTER SIX

'WHERE ARE YOU GOING?'

Harrison's question interrupted Sienna's concentration. He was standing in her garage looking cross.

'Or should that be, where have you been? You're not meant to drive yet, *Doctor.*'

She leaned out the window of her SUV. 'I've been nowhere.' *More's the pity.* 'And I'm going nowhere, *Doctor.*'

'You felt like hanging out in your car for a bit?'

Sarcastic so-and-so. 'You should mind your own business.' He was always interfering. Shoving her door wide, Sienna placed her feet carefully on the ground, not prepared to show him how much she still hurt in most muscles. Nor was she saying what she'd done. Being laughed at would crank her temper up something shocking, though that would be the perfect outlet for all the frustration brought on by a long, tedious day at home.

Those hands that fascinated her beyond reason were now on his hips. Narrow hips on the vee from his wide chest to his— She jerked her head high and clashed with his gleaming eyes.

'You've re-parked the SUV.' There was a lot of amused twitching going on around his mouth.

Too damned shrewd for her good, he was. 'And what if I have?' Wait for it. He was going to burst out laughing any second.

'I didn't park dead straight,' Harry grinned. How was he managing not to laugh?

She hadn't known anyone's eyes could get quite so wide. She hoped it hurt because the way he was looking at her suggested he thought her bonkers. He was probably right. Heat suffused her neck and up into her face. But control was so important. 'No, you didn't.' And that had driven *her* crazy every time she'd brought clothes for the laundry basket out here. She glared at him. *Please don't say anything more.*

Of course he did. It wouldn't be the Harrison she was coming to know otherwise. 'You never just drive in and stop?'

'Every time.' She had it down pat. Line up the right front corner of the bonnet with the edge of the cupboard on the back wall and voila. Perfect.

'I'm getting it.' His shoulders were heaving as he turned away.

'You think?' she asked too quickly.

Harrison came back to her and engulfed her hands in those warm, strong ones she still hadn't got over thinking about. 'I'm not laughing at you. I get that you need to have control over your life. What I don't understand yet is why.'

When he was holding her hands as if she was special all her control disappeared, and she had to fight not to lean in against that expansive chest. He'd said *yet*. Did that mean he wanted to spend more time with her, get to know her a little? Hope flared. Have a fling with him. Now. Quick. That'd mean letting go the bonds she'd put around her libido. Huh? They were already snapping apart, one by one, as Harrison spent more time with her. Hard to pull her hands away when she wasn't ready to let him go, but somehow she managed it. 'It's my way of keeping life on track.'

'Sometimes it's more fun going off track.'

'Sometimes it's downright dangerous.'

Harry stared at her for a long moment. 'I hope not.'

He left her with the shattering sensation that he understood her, knew what made her tick better than she did. Now, *that* was dangerous.

'Well, it's fairly obvious Christmas is just around the corner,' Sienna quipped as she walked into the paediatric ward on Wednesday, the large bag dragging from one hand. Staring around at the decorations, covering every available surface and then some, she laughed. 'Has there been any work done in here?'

Julie, a junior doctor, joined her. 'It's a very serious matter, hanging Santas and coloured glass baubles, I assure you. The kids had a ball.'

'Which has to be good for them. So who's here at the moment?'

'Felicity's still around. She got a mild lung infection after that near-drowning but, being her, she's up and about, refusing to let this setback hold her down.'

'Has she got over her anger at missing out on the school trip?' Fliss was one her favourite patients, not that she could ever admit that out loud, but any time the teen had problems she felt bad for her.

'I think so, but check her out for yourself. Here she comes.'

Felicity was running down the ward, arms outstretched. 'Doc Sienna, you're back. Are you all right? I heard what happened. You look pale and wobbly. Shouldn't you be sitting down?'

Sienna braced herself for impact, but Felicity skidded to a halt just short of a collision. 'Hello to you, too.'

Fliss grinned. 'It's not the same around here without you.'

Water filled her eyes. Sniff. 'Thought I was the dragon lady.'

Fliss's cheeks were full of colour and her breathing only slightly laboured. Definitely ready to go home. 'Everyone needs a dragon on their side. We were told you'd be away all week.'

Sienna winced. 'I've only dropped in to see how everyone's getting on.' Her head still thumped intermittently and she didn't want to push it when decisions about other people's health were at stake. At the same time, staring at her four walls had been slowly driving her insane. The only reprieve had been when Harry dropped in to check up on her or bring a meal he always insisted on sharing. 'And to hand these around. Come on, you can help me.' The ward looked warm and inviting, the sterile white walls no longer glaring. It happened every December yet this was the first time she'd taken serious notice. 'Did you have a hand in the decorating?'

'I helped the little kids make paper chains.' Fliss blushed. She didn't like being seen as a softy by other teens or adults, but she could no more refuse a small child assistance than Sienna could refuse to treat a sick person. 'Some of the chains weren't very good but we put them up anyway.'

'That's what it's all about.' Her fingers itched to straighten the large cardboard star with uneven glitter hanging on the wall. Turning her back on it, she looked into the room opposite, not recognising any of the young patients. 'Want to tell me everyone's name as we go?'

The presents were a hit, and the ward was noisy with laughter and excited shouts. Sienna couldn't stop smiling as warmth threatened to overwhelm her. What a simple thing to do, and yet the rewards were beyond measure.

'Everyone's happy,' Felicity grinned.

'It must be the Christmas spirit.' Something she could do with a dose of at home. She would get a tree and decorations, and it would be a start to livening up her days. The list had come to a grinding halt, tossed in a drawer out of sight. Nothing more had been added, nothing at all completed and ticked off.

Don't sweat the small stuff.

Go away, Harry.

'What do *you* think?' grumped Aiden, fourteen, appendicitis, when she asked how he was feeling, the zing from getting a present gone.

'Definitely ready to go home, I'd say,' she said in an aside to Julie.

'Much to everyone's relief,' the intern smiled. 'Teenagers.'

Toby, ten, another appendectomy. 'Mum's coming to get me after lunch. I can't wait to go back to school.'

'Not this week,' Sienna smiled.

His face fell. 'It's boring at home.'

She couldn't argue with that, so she didn't

try. 'Haven't you got some games to play on your computer?'

'Mum'll make me read books.'

'That's really terrible,' she laughed. What was wrong with her? She never said things like that, always encouraged the kids to read and study and not sit around staring vacantly at their electronic toys.

Julie was looking at her as if she was a stranger. Maybe she was. That accident had rattled her. But changed her? Who knew? 'Right. Who else have we got I need to be introduced to?'

Less than two hours later Sienna hated to admit defeat. She was shattered. Every one of those bruises was protesting, her rib cartilage had a lot to say, and her head was spinning, making it hard to stay upright. 'I'm going home,' she told the staff.

'I'll walk you down.' Dale appeared at her side. 'I need a word with you.'

His tone sounded ominous but when they reached the ground floor all Dale said was, 'Go home and do something for yourself for a change, Sienna. You were beyond exhausted before this accident. It's time to rest and relax, get some energy back. You're not pretty when dragging your butt like you're carrying all the responsibility for the ward.'

'I don't need to be pretty to do my job.'

'Make the most of this time out. Come back refreshed.' Then he was gone, striding back to the lifts.

Sienna stared after the man she'd always believed to be a pushover. When had Dale turned bossy? Another dictatorial man in her life. Two in a week was two too many. The only difference being that she had to keep onside with her boss, whereas Harrison she could and did ignore.

The taxi driver had to wake Sienna outside her apartment. Embarrassed, she clambered out, spilling the contents of her handbag on the road edge, gathering everything up before finally handing him the fare. How had she fallen asleep after Dale's bombshell? Inside she opened windows to let the breeze cool the humid air and found her list to scrawl more ideas that she wouldn't ever act on. Next she headed for the bedroom to fall on top without removing her shoes, already asleep as her head hit the pillow despite the stab of pain from her ribs.

She woke hours later to a delicious smell wafting into her room, and went out to find Harry taking a dish of macaroni and cheese out of her oven. 'Oh, boy, that smells delish.'

'Not bad, eh?'

'You don't do coy, do you?'

'No idea what it means.' He grinned like a naughty boy caught out at something he shouldn't be doing.

'Why am I not surprised?'

'How are you feeling? That was some sleep going on. I could hear the snores out here.'

'He doesn't do diplomacy either,' she muttered.

'Pulling your leg.' He nudged a chair out from the table. 'Take a load off and I'll get the cutlery. This is ready to go.'

'How can I resist such an invitation?' Sienna sank onto the chair, breathing in the rich aroma, and trying to hold her stomach in so it didn't add noise to the scene.

They ate in silence. At least it was companionable. Until Harry said, 'I see you're going to a day spa some time soon.'

Her fork stopped halfway to her mouth. 'You what?'

He shrugged. 'Don't leave it lying around if anything's a secret.' Those full lips tilted up into a wide smile. 'A spa seems innocuous compared to a fling.'

'You think?' Right now a spa was way up there, while a fling wasn't even registering. Not while Harrison was being his usual stroppy self. Setting her fork on the plate, she leaned back in her chair. 'Guess you've never been to a spa, then.'

His eyes widened, and that smile grew. 'I haven't had the need.'

He saw her words as a challenge? *Gah.* Whatever. She was a big girl. 'Another thing to show how different our lives are.' She was backing off, and that surprised her, but then she wasn't used to flirting, usually got cold feet the moment she got close.

Harrison pushed his empty plate aside and leaned back in the chair, his expression now empty of teasing as he watched her. 'We are poles apart, yet we're almost alike in our need to protect ourselves from others.'

The tension that had been tightening over

the last few minutes disappeared. Harrison wound her up, softened her down, all too easily. Thoughtlessly she squeezed his hand, and got zapped by an electric current for her trouble. Or so it felt. Her eyes flicked straight to Harry's, saw the same shock registering in that lightening black-grey.

It wasn't as though she could pull away. If she even tried. Which she didn't. It was more as though they were fused together. Her brain had stopped thinking straight, was entirely focused on the current running between them. Her lungs were acting strange, taking in short grabs of air, pushing it out fast. As for the rest of her body—she was leaning forward, getting closer and closer to Harry. They were standing. How had that happened? Their hands linked, fingers entwined. Breathing the same air, hot air filled with tension and sparks and—

Sienna sighed as Harrison's lips caressed hers. Yes. Exactly what she wanted, needed. No. It wasn't enough. As she pressed forward, her peaked breasts touched his chest. Desire fired through her. Her hips found his. Her stomach clenched, relaxed, clenched. Heat pooled lower. The aches and pains of the last few days receded to a dull background throbbing.

Strong arms wound around her, pulling her into that muscular, masculine body, and she was being kissed thoroughly. Harry left nothing to chance. His mouth claimed hers, his tongue forayed inside, his taste sent over more messages of hazy need. His eyes were open, focused on her. She fell into that gaze, gave over control of her mouth, her body. How could she not?

Harry's arms tightened further as his mouth pressed harder. A groan escaped over her lips. Or was that from Harry? What did it matter? Raising her arms to slide around his neck, she held on as her legs no longer had the strength to keep her standing. As she twisted to get more connection with his chest a serious pain stabbed her right side.

This time her groan wasn't about desire.

Instantly Harry lifted his head, set her back without letting go. Just as well or she'd be staggering around finding her balance. 'I'm so sorry. I shouldn't have done that. I don't want to hurt you.'

'You didn't. I moved badly, did it all by myself.' She wouldn't accept he meant he shouldn't have kissed her. That would be humiliating when she'd finally let go completely to kiss him. She did not want to think that for Harry that was an everyday kind of kiss.

He was staring at the point where her finger touched her mouth. Pulling her hand away, she glanced around the kitchen. Back to reality. The kitchen was ordinary. Reality didn't go with sensational kisses. Kiss. They'd only had one. But what a kiss. Right this minute she'd opt for more over keeping her life on track. Her iron-strong control had been stolen in a moment of need. Her eyes sought Harry again, locked on to him. 'Don't be sorry.'

'I think it's time I headed over the fence.'

Her stomach dropped. So that was how he was going to play it. She wasn't going to beg. They'd shared a moment. Not entirely unexpected—on her part anyway. He both infuriated and intrigued her, and for a few minutes that intrigue had won out. Now she knew what it was like to be kissed by Harrison. Shame it wasn't enough. But it was going to have to be. He was already at the door.

Don't show how disappointed you are.

They did not need to get together for a fling. They were opposites. He was all the things she didn't want in a man. Opposites might attract but that didn't mean they worked out long-term. Look at her parents. Not that she was looking for anything like that. Not even short-term involvement. But some fun wouldn't cause havoc on her heart, would it?

With Harry, it just might.

'Sienna, I'm not running away.' He was back, standing before her, his gaze cruising over her. 'But I don't want to take advantage of you.'

Take advantage of her? 'You didn't. I'm an adult. At least I was last time I looked.' But for a moment back in that kiss she could've been a teenager again.

His finger traced her jawline. 'Believe me, I know. I'm playing safe, okay?'

'Why?' She did safe, not others around her. But he had pointed out they were similar in many ways.

Whipping his hand away, he shoved both in his pockets and stared out the window. 'I don't do permanent.'

'One kiss and you're running from commitment? Excuse me, but that was never on offer.'

'There's something between us. It's been there from the night you walked up my drive. I don't usually stall, but I don't want to hurt you, and I think that would be too easy to do.'

'Trust me, I'm on lock-down. You're a man constantly moving, I'm a woman with my feet firmly fixed on my property. We are never going to have more than some fun, if even that.' Disappointment tasted bitter when it should be gratitude for his not roaring in to stomp all over her feelings. What would it be like to make love with this man? Her blood hummed and her head thumped. She guessed she'd never know.

He turned back to her, then said through the softest, most confusing smile, 'You're not as tough as you make out.'

Forget humming. Her blood was racing with longing. A longing for more than having sex. Longing for making love, not sex. Longing for someone to always be there with a smile like that for her. For a man who understood her far too well with so little to go by. 'Only when I want to be.'

Which is right about now.

But she wasn't saying.

That smile lingered, drumming up inappropriate responses throughout her body. If Harry could read her mind he'd be laughing at her weakness, or he'd be disgusted that she was so easy.

'Sienna.' Her name sounded like honey on his tongue.

'Harry.' Where were they going with this? Actually, she knew. He was right. They'd been headed down this track from the moment they met. She made up her mind in an instant of heat and need. Her lungs filled, drawing in confidence, and a heady mix of man scent. Her shoulders lifted as she laid a hand on his arm. 'Harrison.'

'I haven't been called Harrison so much in years.' The smile widened, his eyes filled with—longing?

Please be that.

'Is that good?' Sienna rose on her toes, ignored the protests from battered muscles, and leaned forward.

Then she was being wrapped in those arms again, Harrison's strength holding her still while he moved closer, shutting out the gap between them—physically if not mentally—to tuck her up against him. There was an incred-

ible gentleness about his movements, an aware-
ness of her bruises that he must've forgotten
when he'd kissed her.

'Don't treat me like a china doll,' she all but
begged.

'Sienna,' he repeated, and put her away from
him. 'I can't. We can't.'

She would not give in to the frustration clawing through her. Not in front of him, at any rate.
'Fine,' she snapped and turned away to fill the
kettle for something to do with her hands before she wrapped them around him and shook
him until he changed his mind.

'I'm attracted to you.' His laugh was terse.
'That's an understatement. But there's the rub.
I'm always moving, never stopping in one place
for long, and nothing's going to change that.
While you...' He stopped.

Turning, she leaned back against the bench.
'I'm in a holding pattern. I go to work, come
home, tidy up, eat, sleep and go back to work.
Occasionally I throw in a bike ride to change
the routine. What has any of this got to do with
not following through on what's between us?'

He pulled a chair out from the table and strad-
dled it, his chin resting on his hand, his eyes

thoughtful. 'It's all part of how I operate. I sign a contract, move to wherever I'm required, see out my time, and find the next contract. I don't stop for anyone or anything.'

When he put it like that her heart squeezed for him. 'You're so self-contained.' That was lonely. Sad, even.

'Aren't you?'

Not quite as much. Her parents were still there for her if she ever asked for help. 'You don't have family to go back to?' He'd never mentioned parents or siblings. Or children. There was also a squeeze for herself at his warning. He wouldn't stop his nomadic lifestyle for her any more than he would for any woman. While it was too early to be thinking about that, she needed to be strong, ready, watching out for her heart, because deep inside warning bells were ringing. Harrison might be the man who could change her perspective on how she lived. Shock rippled through her. Typical. She found a man to tinkle her keys and he was all wrong for her.

'Sure I do.'

What? Family. Right. 'Sharing isn't your thing, is it?' Her voice was harsher than she'd intended, but he never talked about himself.

Had he learned that from his parents? 'Your family not talkers either?' Might as well ask as wonder.

'Most of them don't know when to stop.' It wasn't a joke. When those eyes locked on her she saw anger and bitterness battling for supremacy. 'My mother got pregnant with me when she was nineteen. My grandfather forced her to marry my father by saying he'd disown her if she didn't. Since she had ambitions to take over Granddad's company and the fortune that with it, she didn't argue.'

'Did your father have any say in that?'

'He had plenty of ambition himself. Already working for the company, he saw the opportunities to get to the top and take over. It was a recipe for disaster. There wasn't any love between Mum and Dad.'

'With you caught between them.' She wanted to hug the little boy who'd have been lost in all that, but there was a stop sign blinking out at her. Harry would hate her showing compassion.

'I was stuck right bang in the middle between two warring factions, copping the blame for anything that went wrong. After all, it was my fault they'd had to get married, so it must be my fault the company went through a few bad years; that Granddad wouldn't sign over control to Mum as soon as she wanted it; that the roof leaked. You name it, I caused it.'

Geez, how did any parent do that to their child? Her parents might've given her the craziest start to life but it had been fun and loving, and done with the best of intentions. 'Are you the only child?'

'There's the joke. After my parents married they decided they wanted a family to follow in their footsteps so I have two brothers I adore and would do anything for. My feelings are reciprocated,' he added in a softer voice. 'By them and their wives and kids.'

'So why don't you want what they've got?'

'You seriously think that's going to work? I tried once. Big fail. I refused to be bullied into doing what she wanted.'

'You've been married?'

'Four years and three months. Celia had the same ambitions as my mother—money, power, and never mind who she trod on to get it. Especially me.'

'You didn't see that before you married?'

'You'd think I would've, but no. Celia was so

loving and kind, she'd do anything for me. I fell the whole way. Until I wised up and realised I was being played like a salmon on the line. By then we were married and about to move into a mansion I hadn't even seen when *we* made an offer to buy it.'

'Is that when you called it quits?' This was not the Harrison she'd come to expect when she asked questions. This man still hurt, but seemed to want to get it all out there. With her.

'No, I stayed another two years after that, believing that loving someone was for ever and with everything I had. But finally the give, give, give, without anything in return, got to me, wore me down and turned me sour. It seemed the more I gave the more she wanted.' He stood up to his full height. 'I'd read Celia all wrong right from the start, thought she cared about us, not just her own needs. Should've known better with my history.'

She might've felt intimidated by his height and those broad shoulders that seemed bigger than ever if not for that sadness lurking in the backs of his eyes. This big, strong man had problems that made him hurt on the inside.

'Sure you're not hiding behind this to avoid getting tied down again?'

His eyes widened. 'More than likely, but why would I get married again? Some people are meant to be single, and I'm obviously one of them. Guess my expectations are too high.'

'Doesn't sound like that to me.'

'Then I haven't been clear enough.'

Oh, he'd been clear all right. Like a piece of glass. He wasn't prepared to take another chance on love. She couldn't help nudging him a little. 'You believe those close to you will hold you responsible for everything that happens in their lives, yet it doesn't sound like that when you talk about your brothers.'

'They're different, having grown up with me.'

'You didn't find a middle ground with your wife?'

He grimaced. 'Go for the throat. Exactly what I'd expect from you.'

Her stomach sank. She hadn't intended rubbing him up the wrong way quite that much; the words had just popped out. But she wouldn't retract them. They felt right, so she gave something back and hopefully he'd understand where she was coming from. 'I should know. It's why

I live this ordinary, safe life. I'm afraid to step out of my comfort zone and take risks.'

'What happened to the girl who demanded her parents stop wandering around the country as though there was nothing to linger for?'

'She got tied up with rigorous hours studying and training, and then she fell in love with a man who woke up one morning and decided he didn't love her any more. Apparently she was too cautious and always questioning why they had to move from city to city to chase the perfect job, the best position, when staying in his first job would've seen him at the top by now. He added insult to injury by dumping her for his high-school sweetheart.'

When Harry took a step towards her she held her hands up, palms towards him. 'Don't.' Now he was giving out compassion and it was too much. She didn't need his sympathy, only wanted the one thing he'd withdrawn minutes ago: desire. For her. She had to be grateful he'd stopped when he did. They were on different paths, and the strength of whatever this need between them was could be devastating. There'd be no happy ending, so best to call a halt now.

Heat in the pit of her stomach told her she was lying to herself. So much for starting over. But having a fling, even with her neighbour, wasn't the only thing on the list. She could try something else first.

CHAPTER SEVEN

SIENNA REMOVED HER stethoscope from Felicity's chest. 'You're good to go.'

In typical teenage fashion Fliss shrugged her words away. 'Whatever.' She was back in a bad place. It seemed everyone at school would be raving about the wonderful week on Great Barrier Island and she didn't want to hear any of it.

'Doesn't school finish this week?'

'It's not like we'll be doing any work. It's boring.'

'Have you found a holiday job yet?'

'Duh. I've been in here, haven't I?'

Sienna tipped her head to one side. She wouldn't show pity for her favourite teen. 'I think the internet works in here as well as anywhere.'

'You try getting work when you cough goop like I do. People hate it.'

This day had been coming for a while now. Sienna had spoken to the counsellor about Fliss and knew they'd had a session, but obviously there was still a long way to go. 'Not everyone's like that.'

'Really?' All the hurt from previous rejections spilled into that one word and it took everything she had for Sienna not to cry.

Instead she wrapped her arms around the girl and held her tight. Totally un-doctor-ish, yet about the best medicine she had to offer right now. Anyway, she was off duty this week, and here for a reason. She pulled back. 'What do you want to do when you leave school?'

'Be a lawyer who helps people like me. But I'll be lucky to get work in a warehouse.'

Sienna nodded. She already knew that. This girl had a huge heart and when she wasn't letting her situation get her down was always looking out for others on the ward. 'Okay, Felicity, enough of feeling sorry for yourself. You've shown me your exam results for the year. You are an intelligent girl who can be anything she wants.'

'An astronaut?' There was a lightening in Fliss's expression.

'Since you don't want to be one, I'm not answering that.' Movement down the other end of the ward diverted her attention. Harrison was pushing a trolley with a tiny patient into the ward, and he'd spotted her, his eyes being slits of disbelief. It was none of his business that she was here. Turning away, she tugged her phone out of her bag. 'Don't go anywhere, Fliss. I've got to go make a phone call and then I'll talk to you some more.' She shot into the nearest room and hit Anna's number, and crossed her fingers her friend wasn't with a client. They hadn't been able to set a time for this conversation.

Anna came on the line. 'This still about Felicity or have you decided to sue your bike for taking you over that edge?'

'I could try the manufacturer for a pay-out but I think there'll be a clause somewhere that says any cyclist stupid enough to get distracted by a mental picture of a hot man needs to see a shrink, not demand restorative justice.'

Anna laughed. 'I knew it. He's got to you.'

Sienna closed her eyes and shook her head slowly from side to side. Stupid. She'd fed Anna enough to keep her busy nagging from now until the following Christmas. Lifting her eyelids, she stared through the door to that gorgeous sight of red overalls hiding a perfect body. At least he'd gone back to concentrating on his patient.

'I haven't got all day,' Anna muttered.

'Are you still okay about talking to Felicity?' Every year Anna *found* work for a teenager who had problems in their background in one form or another, and needed money and support. 'Sure.'

'Right, hang on while I take the phone to Felicity.'

Fliss was still sprawled over her bed looking blankly at the ceiling.

Am I doing the right thing?

'Felicity, I've got someone on the phone I'd like you to talk to. Ms McIntosh is a lawyer, so put on your best face.' She handed her phone over to shaky fingers. 'Go on,' she nudged when Fliss just stared at the instrument. 'Introduce yourself.' Then Sienna walked away, and straight into Harry. 'Hi,' she managed around the lump building at the back of her throat.

'Did you get called in?' It was a demand, not a question.

'No.'

'Getting your concussion checked out by someone else?'

'No.' Amy had done that earlier.

'So why are you here and not dealing with that list?' His gaze dropped, cruised down over her fitted sea-green blouse to her even more fitted white jeans. He blinked. 'You're not working, are you?'

'Nope. I came in to arrange for Anna to talk to Felicity about a holiday job in her legal office.' She really wanted to go eavesdrop on Fliss's side of the conversation.

'Why doesn't that surprise me? You doing something kind for a patient outside of here? Sorry for being a prat.' Harrison's gaze turned in the same direction as hers.

'She needs someone to believe in her, someone outside of this place, and not her mother. A stranger who can tell it to her like it is and expect her to pull her weight.'

'Anna will certainly do that.' Harry smiled. 'Watch out.'

Fliss flew towards her. 'Doc Sienna, I've got a job.'

Bracing for the slam coming her way, Sienna laughed. 'You're not meant to run around here.'

Warm arms surrounded Sienna with a thump. 'Thank you, thank you. Ms McIntosh's so nice. She said I can go see her tomorrow after school and she'll show me what I'll be doing.'

Swallowing the stab from her ribs, Sienna warned, 'Anna's a hard taskmaster.' She was also a softie behind that bulldog exterior, but best Fliss worked that out for herself.

'I don't care. I've got a job.' Fliss danced on the spot. 'Woo-hoo.'

A warm hand spread between Siena's shoulder blades. 'Well done, Felicity.'

'Doc Harry? Did you hear that? I'm going to work for Doc Sienna's friend. How cool is that?'

'Very cool.' Harry high-fived Felicity with his other hand.

Slapping his hand, Felicity did a little jig. 'I'm going to ring Mum. She'll be so happy for me. Thanks again, Doc Sienna.' She raced away.

'Fliss?' Sienna called after her. 'My phone?'

'Oops, sorry, forgot.'

With her phone back in her pocket Sienna felt a rush of pure happiness. She'd done something good for this girl that wasn't medical. Now she really should go and do the same for herself.

What brand of cycle would she buy this time? She could top up the insurance pay-out that would turn up in her bank account during the next month and get something swankier than the last one.

'Si?' Harrison stood in front of her. 'Feel like coffee?'

'Haven't you got a helicopter waiting on the roof?'

'We're grounded while the guys fly to the maintenance yard to get something tightened. I said I'd make my own way back to base in an hour.'

'Then coffee sounds good.' Thank goodness she'd put an effort into her clothes that morning, and hadn't chucked on the usual plain skirt and shirt. If the way Harrison's eyes kept giving her the once-over was anything to go by, she'd got her outfit right.

He might be in her life short-term but she would make the most of whatever he had to spare. Starting with coffee. 'Not the hospital cafeteria, please?'

'Wouldn't dream of it, fuss-pants.'

There was a skip in her step all the way to the café along the road from the hospital, but once they were seated with large bowls of steaming cappuccinos in front of them, her excitement died. 'The helicopter wasn't about to fall out of the sky, was it?' Harry being in an accident was not allowed.

'Not at all. We could've operated non-stop all day but it's been quiet and the pilot wanted the job done.'

'What happens if you're needed? When you think it's quiet is usually when the calls start coming in thick and fast.'

Harrison nodded. 'True, but another crew is on standby. They've been doing training exercises all morning so they're up to speed if necessary.'

She could relax. Harry hadn't been in danger. And here he was, sharing coffee in a café— with her. 'I'm going shopping this afternoon.'

'What for?'

'A new bike. Think I'll get something a bit more geared than my last one.'

'So you can fly off the side of a hill faster than last time?' He was laughing but she didn't miss the flicker of concern cross his eyes.

'Good brakes are the first prerequisite.'

'Can you buy focus by the packet?' He sipped his drink.

Heat flooded her cheeks. 'I was focused.'

'Just not on the road.'

'You are such a stirrer, Harrison Frost.' And she liked it despite how he'd somehow figured out he was the cause of her accident, and enjoyed rubbing it in. 'There's nothing wrong with my focus.' Except when he was around. Like now. How long had her phone been ringing? 'Excuse me. I don't usually get calls during the day—it might be important.'

'Go ahead.'

Anna's number showed on the screen, then a text pinged into the box. 'It's Anna, saying she's looking forward to helping Felicity.' Phew. 'Mission accomplished.'

'Go you,' Harry said quietly, all the while watching her with something like care for her in his eyes.

'The humidity has to be at least eighty percent,' Harry grumbled at his own shadow as he slouched up his steps and opened the front door, tipping backward as a wave of hot, heavy air expelled from inside. Heat he could handle, but this humidity did him in. Everyone at work had been complaining while patients had been fractious, unlike their usual grateful selves at being airlifted to hospital.

Opening every door and window wide didn't placate him, nor lighten the sultry heat. Shucking out of his sweaty clothes to pull on a clean set helped his mood a little. The first mouthful of a cold beer helped a lot. He'd been grumpy all afternoon since he'd left Sienna at the café. He hadn't wanted to go back to work and leave her. All because of one kiss.

Kisses weren't meant to unravel a man. At a basic level they were the prelude to sex. At best they were exciting and tempting, and enjoyable. But to knock him off his feet with need and a longing for more—more than sex? It had never happened since Celia; shouldn't be happening now.

He wanted another Sienna kiss.

He needed the follow-through.

He longed to be with her, holding her, touching, talking. Being together.

He had to stay away. Or lose his mind over her, in her.

Sure you haven't already lost it?

Somehow he had to get a grip or the next few weeks were going to be unbearable. First he'd phone Lance and take up the job offer. A year in Melbourne wasn't what he wanted but it would give him something to focus on, because living in his home city wasn't a walk in the park, and would need constant attention to detail to keep out of his mother's firing line. There wouldn't be time to think about a certain sexy, hot, kind, lost lady.

But he still had time to put in here first.

'Harrison, you in there?'

His stomach dived, while his pulse sped up. Straightening his shirt and running his fingers through his hair, he considered hiding in the wardrobe until Sienna got tired of knocking. 'Be right with you.' How was it she brought the child out in him?

'I'm making good on that wine we promised each other while waiting for the chopper,' she called.

'I thought I was bringing you a bottle when you were off your meds.' He stepped into the hall and nearly gasped at the beautiful apparition filling the front doorway. Slender, curvy in the right places, her long auburn hair brushed out over her shoulders, she looked cool and inviting. Should've gone into the wardrobe. This was going to be the longest bottle of wine he'd ever had the pleasure to drink.

'A girl can only wait so long.' Her head shot up, her eyes widened. 'Sorry, that sounded glib. Not me, for sure. But I wanted to say thank you for everything you've done for me since the accident. I really appreciate it.'

She appreciated it? That set him back. He was only doing what he did for anyone needing help, but doing it for—with—Sienna had been different, had drawn him in in ways he was struggling to understand. He certainly hadn't kissed someone he was *only* helping before. 'I like being there for you.' Damn, this sounded so trite. 'Get inside, woman, and let's open that bottle.'

She perked up at his rough tone. 'Inside? You are kidding me.'

'Make that out on the back deck.' Heat of a different sort was taking over and being outside seemed a wise move. He couldn't act on these rampant urges if the other neighbours were looking over the fence. Putting his beer aside, he dug into the cupboard for wine glasses. 'Half the deck's in shade.' Not that that would lighten the air.

'For the record, I'm off all medication now.'

'That's good news. Make yourself at home while I grab some cheese and crackers.'

The sweetest laughter exploded behind him. Jerking around, he couldn't believe what he was seeing. Sienna laughing so hard her body shook. 'Hello? What's so funny?' She looked so lovable he nearly reached for her. Nearly. The old voice that had played the warning tune all his life—don't get close, don't expect her to love you for who you are—sprang into life just in time. It took a couple of minutes to get a reply and by then mascara had done a number on her face.

'Your Christmas tree.' She wiped her hand across her cheeks.

'I like it. Especially the scent of pine.' They'd never been allowed something so uncontained at home, had had to have the perfect lines that only false trees came with. 'It's random.'

'Not one branch is in sync with another. The ends all droop, pine needles are already covering the floor. There's a bend in the trunk making it look drunk.'

'Probably is, considering I was having a beer at the time I put it up.'

'None of the decorations match, and there are big gaps where more are needed. It's a mess and I love it.' She leaned closer and pointed. 'There's a Santa with only one leg.'

'The reindeer will get him to the chimneys.'

'Come with me.'

His hand was gripped in a vice made of slim, warm fingers and he was being dragged out and down the drive, up the matching one and inside Sienna's apartment. 'See?' She pointed through to her lounge.

His stomach knotted. A fake Christmas tree all perfectly aligned, no branches going in all directions, and the decorations—well—they were gold and red, perfectly matched, placed equidistantly apart. There were no Santas with a leg missing, or bent stars the family who normally lived next door must have made with their kids. It was fake. 'I guess there are Christmas trees and then there's mine.' She so was not the woman he needed in his life, if he ever went off the rails entirely and fell in love. Sienna had some attributes he'd never be able to live with.

Yet Sienna was grinning as if this was the funniest thing to happen to her. 'We are so different, you and I.'

'We certainly are,' he agreed around the lump forming in his throat. He didn't want that, but nor could he deny the truth of it. 'At least we like the same wine.'

'You're showing me up again for the control freak I've become.'

Why was she looking so happy about that? She wasn't letting go because of him, was she? Where would that leave him when he needed at least one of them being sane and sensible in twenty days' time? Because he could feel it in his veins, his gut, his everywhere, that he was losing grip on reality. 'I never set out to do that.'

'Just being you did it. But you know what? It's cool. Today I broke out, bought a tree for the first time. And a new bike. And knocked on your door with a bottle of wine.'

'That's quite a day.'

'Yep, and there's one thing left to do.' She stalked over to the tree.

'No, Sienna, no. That's who you are.' She'd regret this tomorrow and he might get the blame.

Removing three red baubles, she randomly placed them elsewhere. 'Got any Santas left over in your place?'

'There's one I think a dog might've chewed.'

'It's mine for the next three weeks.' Then she hesitated, her eyes going to those three baubles, and for the first time he'd ever seen she nibbled her bottom lip. 'I can do this. I am a mixed-up puppy, for sure, but I can do it.'

Harry had to. He just had to. He could not stand that uncertainty suddenly reflected in her eyes and her voice. Three long strides and he was in front of her, wrapping his arms around her. 'Maybe, but mixed up's better than standing back and not getting involved.' His chin rested on the top of her head, his nose enjoying the apple scent of her shampoo. Then he heard his words. He didn't do involvement, so why had he put it out there that Sienna should?

'You reckon?' she asked against his chest.

Forget involved or anything else that might lead to trouble. Right now, holding Sienna was magic. 'Yeah.' He really, really did. Which led to the next thing he could no longer avoid. 'Mind if I kiss you?'

'You have to ask?'

'Not really.' Her body had somehow moulded to his, her breasts were rising and falling faster than they'd been moments ago. No, he didn't need to ask if she wanted it, but he needed to make sure she'd thought past the desire spiking in her eyes right now. 'Sienna?'

'We didn't even get to open the wine.' Her smile was impish.

'You were planning on seducing me?' For once he couldn't find a reason to argue with that.

A blush crept into her cheeks. 'Sort of. I think. Who cares?' Then she gave him his first full-blown smile and he was lost. He'd give her anything she asked for right at that moment.

'I don't.' His mouth came down over hers, and there was nothing else to be said. It was true—actions spoke louder than words. She tasted wonderful, her lips soft and demanding, her body pressing ever harder against his growing need.

And then there wasn't room for thinking, only feeling, falling into heat and need, wanting more. The kiss deepened, became long and hot and laden with all the things he'd dreamed of kisses being and hadn't found.

In the bedroom—how had they got there? Walked? Crawled?—Harry continued kissing her while his fingers worked at the buttons of her blouse. Her fingers plucked unsuccessfully at the stud of his jeans. Giving up with an exasperated growl, she ran the palm of her hand down over his arousal.

He wasn't going to last the distance if she kept that up. Ladies first. 'Let me,' Harry groaned through gritted teeth. In an instant his jeans were on the other side of the room, his shirt landing on top. Then he was tugging her blouse over her head, and pausing, his eyes scanning her beautiful breasts held in white lace. Breasts that he had to hold, to lick, to… 'Are you sure?' Those bruises may be fading but they were still real. He would not hurt her, would somehow manage to hold on to his almost out-of-control need for her if there was the slightest chance of inflicting even the smallest amount of pain.

Even as she grabbed her blouse from his hand to place it neatly on the chair, she was pulling his head close with her other hand so he had to touch that tormenting cleavage with his mouth. 'Don't you dare stop now. I want this.'

'So do I.' He began to kiss a trail of featherlight touches starting just below her ear, down her neck, and finally reaching that magnificent swell of her breasts. He breathed and tasted and touched. Sienna. Ah, Sienna. From the first time she'd approached him he'd had to have her, and now all his reservations flew out the window on a wave of pure desire and delight and wonder. This went way further than he'd been before. He couldn't get enough contact, wanted his whole body to know the experience of Sienna; her skin, her fingertips, her breath. Her heat and warmth and dampness.

Then her fingers were caressing his skin, moving down to his abdomen, and further down to encircle his manhood, and he was lost against her, his need throbbing as he touched and caressed and finally had her begging for release. He held her at the peak, knew her throbbing need, wanted her to scream her release.

'Harrison.' His name shot across her swollen lips in a long, sexy gasp right before shudders tore through her body, setting his already heated body on fire.

And then they were on the bed, Harry above her, his eyes locked on hers as he touched her again before joining her intimately. When Sienna attempted to pull him down onto her body he wasn't having it, held himself above, aware of those bruises and her ribs. And then he forgot everything else as he lost himself in Sienna.

Unbelievable. His lungs were dragging in short gasps of air, while his blood rampaged around his veins. As for his heart, it didn't seem to know how to cope, just squeezed intermittently. He'd never breathe normally again, never be able to stand upright. Every muscle felt incapable of tightening, his toes unable to wriggle. It couldn't get better than this.

Somehow Harry lifted away to lie on his back and reach for Sienna, to hold her carefully before lowering her over his body as gently as possible, careful not to knock her ribs.

Tears appeared in the corners of her slumberous eyes. 'I'm not fragile.'

Hell, he knew that. She'd just given him the most amazing sex he could remember.

It wasn't sex, Harry. That was making love.

Those short breaths stuttered, stalled, made his chest hurt. He didn't do making love.

Want to take it back?

No. Never. His hands splayed across the soft

mounds of her butt. He was a goner. The words leaked from his mouth in a bemused whisper. 'Ah, Sienna, what have we started?'

CHAPTER EIGHT

'I CAN'T ANSWER THAT.' Sienna whispered her reply. Making love with Harrison was out of this world more than she could ever have imagined. 'I only know I want to do it again.' And again. Did she mention again?

'I'm more than happy to oblige, ma'am.'

Elbowing him in the ribs, she laughed. 'Cheeky.' Then she threw herself over him and obliged right back.

'Sun's going down. Let's go over to my deck, open a wine and eat some steak.'

'Spoken like a true man.'

'Lady, if you haven't figured that out by now then I've been wasting my time.'

Another laugh spilled over her lips. She'd been giving a lot of those lately. 'I'll make a salad.' Someone had to make some pretence at being healthy.

After some wine and barbecued steak with fries and salad they made their way inside and down to Harry's room to try out his bed. It worked perfectly. Sienna only hoped the remaining weeks before he left were enough to sate her appetite. And if they weren't? She wasn't going there. Why spoil a wonderful interlude with negative thoughts? At the back of her mind she knew this was a short-term fling and it would come to an end, but only then would she deal with the consequences. Now was about sharing meals and talking about the most ridiculous subjects, like what to wear when on a lion safari in Africa—she had no intention of going to Africa—and making love long and slow into the late evening. She reached for him and forgot everything else.

When Harry got up to go to work in the morning Sienna had headed through the fence to shower and plan her day. Now she was heading back over the harbour bridge to a mall to do some serious shopping after an eventful morning.

On the console of her car the phone hummed. A parking space was only metres ahead, which she snagged. 'Hey, Anna, how's things?'

'Just thought I'd let you know Felicity's working out well. How she copes with that CF all the time is beyond me. She's one tough cookie.'

'I know. It comes from having to be.' Sienna was thrilled Felicity and her friend were getting on well, and that Anna had no complaints about the girl's work efforts. It had been a stroke of genius putting them together, and there hadn't been a moment of doubt.

'So, how's it going with Mr Tall, Dark and Gorgeous?' Anna always switched subjects fast, said it was how she kept the opposition on their toes in court.

Denial was a waste of time. It was this woman's job to see through the most experienced liars. 'Great. And that's all I'm saying.'

'That's all I wanted to know.' Anna laughed.

Sienna wasn't buying it; she knew Anna too well. But she'd go along with her for now. 'You decided what you're doing Christmas Day yet?'

'Is he as good as he looks?'

No such thing as lead-in time. Nor was there any chance she was answering that. She mightn't be a lawyer but she could play the game. 'You coming to my place or going to your cousin's?'

'Millicent's. Sorry, but the whole family will

be there and the pressure's going on already. I'd better make an appearance, but have a spare bottle of wine in case I need to beat a hasty retreat.' Anna adored her family, but couldn't cope with the overwhelming love they dumped on her, saying it made her claustrophobic.

'Your favourite Pinot Gris, no less.' It was also her preferred choice, so it wasn't hard to please Anna.

'Well, is he?'

'Not answering.'

'I'll take that as a yes, then.' Then Anna turned serious. 'I'm glad you're having some fun; just don't get too involved, okay?'

'No chance. He's leaving at Christmas. It takes longer than a few weeks for me to let anyone get close.' Except she was already in deep, wanted more with Harrison than a fling.

Sure this has nothing to do with amazing sex and a hot man stewing your brain? Or has that knock on the head done some permanent damage?

'I'm not so sure about that. You might've met your match.'

Only a close friend could get away with that. 'I think it was the sitting on the side of the hill in the middle of a storm and seeing my life fly before my eyes that made me take a chance, but I'm still in control.' Sienna hung up and stared out the window. Wasn't she? Harrison wasn't into telling her much about himself, and that irked the more time she spent with him.

He hadn't answered when she'd enquired where his next job would be, and, not wanting to upset him, she'd left it alone. It wasn't as though knowing where his next job was would alter what was happening between them. From what she understood, his next contract could be anywhere. That much she did know about the man, and she really knew it as that was how her father operated.

She'd have liked to use Anna as a sounding board as she worked her way through the little she knew, but no matter how close they were, how much they knew about each other, she wasn't discussing Harry's personal life behind his back.

Harrison had issues with relationships and she could certainly understand why, but when he'd talked about his brothers his shoulders hadn't tightened, his mouth hadn't flattened, and there'd been love in his eyes. So he did have some good, honest relationships in his life. Why not try another one with a woman? Whatever had gone down between him and his parents kept him away from Melbourne and his brothers, but there had to be more to it. No one upped sticks and left without good reason.

Dad did it, and has never stopped, apart from my five years' gift.

Her father had been on a mission to get away from his father, to be the artist he was and not the lawyer his parent expected.

But that didn't mean Dad had to keep moving from place to place.

He could've settled anywhere. Couldn't Harry stop in one place, make a home for himself where he'd create a circle of friends, get a job that he'd see through the years, not the weeks or months?

Harry, Harry, Harrison. He was in her head no matter what. She smiled, rolled her shoulders, and tugged her phone from her pocket to call him. 'Hi, how's your day going?'

'Up and down. Four call-outs so far, which is kind of hectic.' Surprise shaded his question, 'What about you?'

Was he worried about why she'd rung? 'I

went out to the aero club to make enquiries about learning to fly, got taken on a trial flight, booked my first lesson for Monday, and soon I'll hit the mall. Just thought I'd say hello, that's all.' That's all? It was momentous for her, probably mundane for many people, but then she didn't do hot sex with a man she didn't know very well. That had switched on all kinds of emotions; the strongest being happy.

'You were serious about learning to fly? I thought that was a passing notion to fill in time while stuck on that hill.'

'It's on the list.'

'Yes, I saw that,' he admitted through a laugh. 'Are you going to do everything you wrote down?'

'Seems like it.'

'Have you ticked off the one we've been working on?'

Heat spilled into her cheeks. 'It was tempting. I even had a red felt pen in my hand, but I chickened out.'

Have a fling with a hot man—that had happened. So far a one-night stand, but who knew what the coming days would bring? As for ticking that off the list, it kind of cheapened the ex-

perience, so she'd put the cap back on the pen
and dropped it in the drawer.

'Got to go. There's been a crash on the Brin-
duan's.'

'Catch you later.' How cool was that? Talking
to Harrison came easily, and as far as she could
tell he hadn't been annoyed with her phoning.
They'd even talked about last night in a round-
about way and she still felt comfortable with
him.

On the footpath a woman was walking two
dogs on leads and a pang of longing hit Sienna.
Owning a dog would be fun, special, a pet to
love and rush home to at the end of the day.
And not fair on the animal with the long hours
she kept. It wasn't even worth putting that one
on the list. Nor was a pet a man replacement.

With all the moving around, then the years
of studying, she'd never had a dog or a cat. Not
even a pet rock. Her father had always said no
when she'd asked for a puppy. They'd lived how
he decreed, and that was that.

*It's in his bones, the need to continually move,
never sit still. You can't change him. Which
means you probably can't change Harry. If you
wanted to.*

She didn't like the idea of losing Harry from her life, but she also wasn't about to make a fool of herself by asking that he change his lifestyle. Nor would she ever go back to the nomadic way of her childhood. She just couldn't.

Despite the sun pelting down on her arms, a sudden chill enveloped her. Had she got in too deep too quickly? Was she going to be able to wave him goodbye and not fall apart?

She had no choice.

She had to make the most of the days and nights she had. That was all. Suck it up and enjoy; laugh and have fun. This was starting to sound as though she cared too much for Harrison. Cared? Loved? Her heart skittered. She loved Harrison? As in give-up-the-life-she'd-made-for-herself-to-be-with-him love? To follow him anywhere? No. All her adult life she'd believed she would never do that for anyone, and that hadn't changed even if her lawns were mown in circles now and not straight lines. This wasn't love. More like deep friendship with benefits. *Gah.* That sounded terrible. Strange how she couldn't come up with a better description though.

* * *

Harry simply couldn't get Sienna out of his system, not even after the long, hot night they'd shared. From the moment he'd left her to go to work the hours had dragged, become laborious. He wanted more of what they'd shared throughout the hours in his room. Bad for the future. Good for now.

At least Sienna would be at home when he finished his shift, and they could continue working this *thing* out of their systems. She'd surprised him when she phoned, but he'd also been surprised at how good that had made him feel. Like he was a part of something he had never had. Seriously? A simple phone call and he was all hot and flustered? Who knew where they were headed with this…? This fling? Interlude? Getting together. It wasn't something permanent. They both understood they were opposites, wanted very different futures, so this had to be about having fun and using up some hormones. Right?

'Three minutes to destination.' The pilot's confident voice sounded in his headphones.

'Roger.' Where did Roger come from? Why didn't everyone say okay, or right, or Gerry?

Harry shrugged and looked out the window, his head space a mix of the serious and ridiculous since making love with Sienna the first time. And something else he couldn't name. Couldn't, or wouldn't? Afraid to look the truth in the eye? 'What truth would that be?' he asked under his breath.

Connor tapped his arm. 'Over to the left.'

The state highway stretched north and south through dairy farms as far as he could see, with a small school directly below. The playground was devoid of children, while three adults stood on the perimeter, one holding high a home-made wind sock for the pilot. 'No sign of the bee swarm that struck our patient,' Harry tossed over his shoulder.

'Unless it had found a suitable tree, it wasn't likely to hang around. The kid was lucky to only receive a few stings.'

'More than enough to go into anaphylactic shock.' Harry returned to staring out at the rapidly approaching scene, breathing deep, in and out, slowly, calming the sudden but familiar fear that he wouldn't be good enough for the child relying on him to save his life. Once the rotors slowed he'd be okay and the dread would recede, but until then he had to wait out this insecurity. He'd never worked out where it came from, but presumed it was from never getting anything right for his mother. Now he accepted this aberration as part of who he was when in doctor mode. Could be it had made him stronger as a doctor, helped him to see more clearly the priorities and how to stabilise patients successfully.

Whichever, it made him more vigilant, sharper, more connected with his patient for the time they were together, whether it was minutes or hours.

Hours. On a hill. Together. Time. Sienna. A sleepless night, her messed-up bed, his messed-up bed, a driving sense of time disappearing on him way too rapidly.

'One minute.'

Harry stood up, moved to sit on the edge at the door, his pack at hand, feet planted on the bar used to disembark. 'Here we go.'

The wheels touched the ground with only a nudge. The rotors were already slowing. Harry slipped to the grass and bent over low before running across to the men and woman at the edge of the playground. One man was pointing to a building and running in that direction. Harry charged after him. 'Is this boy known to have an allergy to bees?' he asked once within earshot.

'No, but we have two children who are so we recognised the symptoms and have the means to administer an antidote. One was administered within minutes of our realising what was going on, but Tommy's not reacting as we hoped.'

'Any known allergies?' he asked as they reached the boy, whose face was swollen to the point he couldn't open his eyes.

'Nothing on his records.'

'Hello, Tommy. I'm a doctor and I came on the helicopter to help you, so don't be afraid. Have you ever had bee stings before?' Find a country kid who hadn't, but Harry liked to start softly with little ones. He asked over his shoulder, 'Have the parents been told?'

'Yes, but, as luck would have it, they're in town. They're waiting there to see if you're taking Tommy to hospital.'

Harry nodded. That wasn't the best-case scenario. He preferred a parent to accompany children but it was what it was. 'Tommy, I'm going to give you an injection to help with the bee sting. Is that okay?'

'Will it hurt?' the boy asked in gasps, his shortness of breath another confirmation of an anaphylactic shock. 'The other one did.'

'If it does I'll buy you an ice cream when you're better.' He'd set himself up to fork out for a treat but that tiny smile the kid was giving back was worth it. 'First I'm cleaning your skin with a wipe.' He tore the packet open and sterilised Tommy's upper arm, then prepared the dose of epinephrine. 'What's your favourite flavour?'

'Chocolate with extra chocolate buttons.'

'That's mine, too.' Done, and not a murmur. 'There you go, sport.'

'You did it already?' The kid's face fell, and the gasps were harder. 'I didn't know.'

Harry patted his hand. 'That's because you're brave. Let's make it a double-sized cone.'

'Really? Thanks, mister.'

Harry picked up the boy's hand, began rubbing the back to bring the veins to the fore. 'One more prick, Tommy, so we can get fluid into you.' This wouldn't be so simple. The needle was bigger, but there were good veins to work with.

Sure enough, Tommy howled. 'Ow, that hurts!' His face fell. 'Do—do I still get my ice cream?'

'Of course you do, sport. But first you're going for a helicopter ride. Ever been in one of those?'

'No, but I want to.'

'Then let's get you on a stretcher and we'll go for a fly. I need you to lie still and not talk unless we ask you questions, okay?'

The boy nodded, his breathing still laboured, so the less he spoke the easier on his lungs.

'Do they breed them tough out here or what?' Harry said to Connor when the cannula was in place.

'I reckon. The kid could show some adults a thing or two.'

While Connor strapped Tommy onto the stretcher, Harry approached the teacher. 'Can you inform the parents Tommy has had a moderate reaction, but he's doing fine. We'll take him to North Shore Hospital. They can meet us there.'

North Shore, not Auckland and Sienna's

ward. Not that she'd be at work, but even landing at that hospital had him thinking Sienna.
An enigma. She managed to wind him up
something shocking when no one else could,
but more and more he was starting to see behind the control she exercised over herself and
everything around her to the kind, fun-loving,
gentle yet tough woman she was. As if she was
deliberately letting him in one step at a time.

Only that morning when he'd left his bed to
get ready for work he'd tripped over clothes
lying on the floor. *Her* shirt and skirt. Unheard
of. He recalled the first day he'd gone in to
make sure she was all right and get her some
food, she'd got up and made her bed, every corner tucked exactly the same, not a wrinkle in
sight, the two stacks of pillows up against the
headboard identical.

Last night had been the antithesis to that Sienna. There'd been no control whatsoever when
she made love with him. She'd touched him
sensually and with confidence, equally she'd
received his touches and strokes, and when she
came it was with abandon. Heat was firing in
his veins just recalling last night. He needed
something else to concentrate on if he wasn't

going to look stupid when they landed at the hospital.

Harry checked out his patient. 'The flying's fun, isn't it?'

Tommy nodded, his lips pressed firmly together, not saying a word.

Harry grinned. 'Be better if you could see out, but I don't want you sitting up. You'll have to go flying again another day.' This time he got a bigger nod.

Glancing at his watch, Harry sighed. Four hours before he knocked off, if that happened on time, which often didn't in this job. All day he'd been counting the minutes, checking the time way too often, which only made the day drag ever slower. Last night after making love with Sienna in the early hours, he'd lain beside her until she fell asleep, only to give himself a lecture about letting her fill his head and waken his body in lasting ways. Finally unable to resist, he'd rolled toward her and tucked against her soft skin and nuzzled into her neck—and stayed with her until the sun came up. A first. On their first night together.

Bad move. Impossible-to-avoid move. Scary. She'd told him very little about herself.

Oh, and he had given her a long account on his family and past, had he?

But he knew enough to believe her desire to hold sway over everything possible had been brought about by her childhood. Waking up every morning wondering where she'd be when she climbed back into bed at night time would be hard for anyone to cope with, let alone a child without siblings or friends to share the disappointments with. It made his blood boil to think of the young Sienna missing out on friendships and stability because her father liked to gad about the country as the inclination took him. Why hadn't her mother stood up to him?

'We're here,' Connor told Tommy. 'Doc Harry will take you inside.'

Good idea. Then he might stop thinking about Sienna for five minutes.

'You joining the gang at the pub tonight?' Connor asked after they'd dropped Tommy off.

It was Friday and a few beers at the end of the shift was mandatory. 'Might give it a miss tonight.'

Connor's head tipped back. 'You coming down with something?'

Lust. Needs. A great woman who looked amazing in black lace knickers and bra. Yeah, he liked coming down with her. 'Just got a couple of things on.' Such as sharing a meal and going to bed, and not getting up until the sun came up because he liked having Sienna's legs wrapped around his all night. 'Oh, forget it. Count me in.' They weren't joined at the hip. He didn't want that kind of relationship. He had to be free to come and go as he pleased, not trying, and no doubt failing, to keep someone else happy all the time. He had to fight this, not give in to the need clawing through him, making him giddy. 'I've got a phone call to make first.'

Back on the ground Harry loaded up with kits and gear and sauntered into the hangar, his phone at his ear. 'Hi, Sienna. You spend all your hard-earned dosh at the mall?'

'Had to take out a loan. You finished for the day yet?'

'Just knocking off and going for a beer with the gang. Not sure what time I'll be home.' Damn but if that didn't sound like a husband tied at the apron strings. 'We might head into town afterwards.'

'Sure. Have a good time. Might see you over

the weekend.' If that wasn't disappointment coming over the airwaves at him then he was a monkey's cousin.

But he had to go with what he'd started, as they weren't in a relationship that did the 'where are you, why aren't you home with me?' stuff. 'Okay.' At least he'd told her, not just not turned up even when they hadn't made arrangements to get together.

'Maybe.'

Ouch. Exactly why he didn't want to get in too deep. He'd thought—make that hoped—they were on the same page, understanding there was no future together. Had Sienna got too caught up in the shared moments that she'd forgotten they weren't right for each other outside of a few hours in bed?

Oh, and you're not feeling the pinch? Not starting to wonder how you're going to leave without a backward glance come Christmas?

Definitely time for another phone call. One that'd get him out of the hot water swirling at his knees, his gut, his heart. His heart? No way.

Then do something about it—stop procrastinating.

His finger hit Lance on speed dial. Using his

shoulder to hold the phone tight against his ear, he packed syringes into the kitbag and listened to the ringing tone, and waited, and waited, until the answering service came on. Tossing the phone aside, he denied the ping of relief that metallic voice had brought him. He needed to get his next job sorted, and the Melbourne position was excellent, would look good on his CV. He could make a life outside the hospital knowing it wasn't for ever. Face it, he told himself, there still weren't any other jobs waving at him, unless he made the call to go further offshore. Singapore, Hong Kong even. Or the States. He'd never worked that far afield and wasn't that keen. He liked Australasia, felt he belonged in either country. But getting away on or before the twenty-fifth was essential. Christmas with Sienna would be going a step too far, cementing another foundation in their relationship that suggested there'd be more foundations to follow.

Christmas was a time for family and close friends. The speed with which he and Sienna were approaching this *friendship* was frightening and there didn't seem to be any brakes in sight. It could go further than he wanted.

Hurting her was not an option either, though the pressure was lessened knowing she was of the same thought process. Not that it had been put in words exactly, but they both *knew*.

Damn it all. He was a mixed-up bag of needs. 'You taking your heap of metal to the pub, Connor?' he called through the door into the staff kitchen.

'Yep. You want a lift?'

'Too right.' Better to leave his vehicle in the security of the flying rescue base than parked outside the pub all night. 'I feel a bender coming on.' Anything to drown out images of Sienna sprawled beneath him, her head tipped back in ecstasy. Her blistering smiles. Then the picture of her laughing over the differences between their Christmas trees. Oh, yeah, he had some serious forgetting to do.

But when Connor offered him the use of his beach house and fishing boat in Coromandel for the weekend he forgot all about forgetting and instead began dreaming of two whole days—and a night—away with Sienna doing things he enjoyed, and hopefully she did too. 'Thanks, man, I'd like that.' Fishing was his favourite occupation outside of work, and boats, being a part of the scene, were up there too. But higher on the scale for his excitement was Sienna. When he was meant to be remaining uninvolved, all he could think about was getting closer. He had it bad for her. Not that he was admitting that. No way.

CHAPTER NINE

'GET UP, LAZYBONES.'

'Harry?' Sienna forced her eyelids up.

'Don't tell me there's another man you allow to walk into your bedroom when the mood strikes him.' Gentle fingers teased at her hair, lifted it off her shoulder, ran strands over his palm.

'I wasn't aware I allowed you to do that. You kind of made yourself at home.' She reached for his hand. 'Not that I'm complaining.'

'Good. Now get up, will you?'

'Where did you come from? I didn't miss something, did I?' Like kisses and hands and making love? He hadn't called in when he returned home last night—at five past ten, and she'd been miffed—but he was here now and she didn't want to waste time complaining.

'Maybe.' His wicked grin sent a shiver down her spine.

'What time is it?'

'Five thirty.' He was dressed in shorts and a tee shirt that did nothing to hide the muscles underneath. His hair was a mess, and stubble highlighted his stubborn chin.

Reaching for him, she growled, 'I'm not getting up at this hour.' Not when she'd read an unputdownable book till two in the morning. 'Climb in here with me.' It was good she'd never asked for her key back.

He took three steps back. 'Uh-uh. No can do.' There wasn't even any regret in those dark eyes. Make that not much. 'We're going away for the weekend, and the sooner we're on the road the better.'

Now she was fully awake. Did Harry just say *they* were going away? Tossing the bedcover aside, she sat up. 'Tell me more.'

'Do you like fishing?'

Her nose screwed up. 'As in, getting all stinky and icky?'

'Yes, that kind of thing.'

'Not really.' Hold on. An image of her and Dad in a dinghy with lines over the sides while they talked about anything and everything came to mind. Warmth trickled through her. A good Dad moment. The meal of battered snapper afterwards hadn't been bad either. 'Okay, maybe a little bit.'

'Good, because we're off to Coromandel, where we have the use of a bach and boat for two days, starting now. Let's go.' He was already heading out the door. 'I've thrown some food in a chilly bin and we can stop in Thames township for anything else.'

'I haven't said I'm coming.' But she was already on her feet, heading for a quick shower to wash the sleep out of her eyes. A weekend away with Harry was right up there, was already negating that residual sense of let-down from last night.

Harry turned at the end of her hallway, a grin on his far too handsome face. 'But you are. Even if I have to toss you over my shoulder and haul you out to the four-wheel drive.'

Oh, yes.

Sinking against the wall, she laughed. 'Come on, then.'

He stepped towards her.

She beat a hasty retreat to the bathroom. Her body needed a wash, while her head needed time to absorb this sudden change of plan. Not that she'd intended doing more than going to the market this morning.

Amazing how quickly a girl could shower, apply make-up and pack an overnight bag when she put her mind to it. Make that when she was excited about what might lie ahead. Lie, as in bed, and having out-and-out fun without the restraints of having to remember to go to work or clean the kitchen.

Harry must've been feeling the same as there was a load of humming going on as he backed down the drive. 'Five to six. I like your action, woman.'

'I'll need a caffeine fix before too long,' she warned while suppressing a smile. Couldn't let him think he could charge into her house, take over her weekend, and not have to pay in any way. 'Probably breakfast as well. Not a pot of yoghurt on the run, either.'

'Some women are so darned demanding.' He said that without a trace of annoyance. Further progress, and promising. This weekend was going to be something else.

Laughter bubbled up Sienna's throat. 'You wouldn't want a wimp, would you?'

'Sometimes they have their advantages. But

mostly, no.' His hand touched her thigh briefly before returning to the steering wheel. 'So here's the deal. This bach's in Coromandel township itself, and there's a boat ramp near by. The weather's meant to be perfect for fishing. And if it's not we have other ways of making the most of our time.'

She could only smile through the images that that conjured up, none of which had anything to do with fishing.

'I hope you packed shorts and more of that sexy underwear, and little else.'

'Spoil all my surprises, why don't you?' There'd been a lingerie shop in the mall that she hadn't been able to walk past yesterday, so she'd added to the one decent set of black lace she owned with a red set, a cream one and a black chemise that had *her* blushing. Probably overkill, but she was making the most of having Harry in her life for this short time.

'To hell with fishing. Let's go straight to option two.'

'It shouldn't have been second anyway,' she gave him with a nudge in his ribs with her elbow.

'Good point.' Harry drove onto the southern

motorway. 'Do you know the way or should I use the GPS?'

'I haven't been to the Coromandel since I was ten, but it's straightforward. Should be sign-posted all the way, since the peninsula is popular with locals and tourists alike.'

'You can recall your age at every place you and your parents stopped?'

'All part of keeping control over my life.' Had she always been a control freak? Mostly. It wasn't an adult habit she'd learned after settling in Auckland. Waking up every morning as a child reciting the name of the latest location they were staying at, reminding herself of her age, the plans for the day: all part of dealing with whatever would come her way over the next twenty-four hours.

'So when you lived in Thames, did you go fishing?'

'Down there everyone goes fishing.'

Breakfast in Thames township was long and leisurely. Sienna hadn't felt so relaxed in for ever. It was as though she and Harrison had always been together, the conversation easy and ordinary with no hidden agendas. She had to keep pinching herself to know it was real, that she wasn't dreaming. What residual tension still hovering in her system disappeared somewhere between the eggs Benedict and the strong coffee.

Finding their accommodation was straightforward, Coromandel having one main street. The bach was small and simply furnished. 'It's got everything we need,' Harry said as he dumped their overnight bags on the floor of the bedroom, his gaze fixed on the not so large bed. 'We can make this work.' He reached for her.

Sienna stepped close, plastering her overheated body to his, her nipples tight and sensitive against his chest, her thighs taking in the heat of his, her core hot and moist as his hardness pressed into her belly. 'We don't need a bed,' she whispered.

'Not every time,' Harry whispered back against her ear, his sharp breaths setting the skin on her neck alive with desire.

Sienna closed her eyes and tipped her head back to expose her throat for those lips that could send her into a frenzy with little effort. Harrison was irresistible. When he made love to her it was as though she became a different woman, one who could let go the locks on her self-control; could just enjoy; was able to give and take without questioning herself about everything, about if she was doing the right thing. Desire rocked throughout her as she gave herself over to Harry.

'So much for an early start to the fishing.' Harry grinned at her as he pushed the boat off the trailer into the water.

'Don't for one moment think I'm ever going to come second to a fishing rod and bait.' Sienna wagged a finger at him. 'Just remember there are more lacy pieces to keep your mind off that.' The simple but creative cream bra and G-string she'd put on back at home had had him agog earlier.

'Get in, woman,' he growled. 'Before I change my mind and haul your sexy butt back to the bach.'

Again she laughed, and clambered aboard the aluminium boat and used the pole tucked in the side panel to hold the boat in place while Harry parked the four-wheel drive and trailer on the roadside. Even going out fishing with Harry was fun. He was making her see everyday life in a totally different light, and that was special, if not a little scary. But she wasn't going to let the scary encroach today. It would spoil a wonderful time with someone she was caring about maybe a little too much.

Harry headed for the spot marked on a map by a cross that Connor had given him when he'd handed over the keys for everything. 'A GPS would be handy,' he muttered as he stared back to shore to line up the points marked in blue on the map.

'Excuses, excuses. If you don't catch a fish you're going to blame the lack of a GPS.' Sienna laughed as she dropped her baited hook over the edge, let the line out firmly and moved quietly so as not to disturb any cruising snapper, before sitting down on the edge of the boat to wait. 'Let me show you how it's done.'

'I'm told catching snapper takes patience and skill.' Those wide shoulders lifted and fell back into place.

Even out here in the hot sun, bobbing on the water, holding a rod, she could get distracted far too easily by his physical attributes. 'You think I don't have either requirement?' she asked with her tongue pressing out a cheek.

One way of holding some control over the feelings watching Harry engendered.

'I am so not setting myself up for that fall,' he chuckled. 'I've never caught one before.'

'I might have. I don't remember, but I do recall being told not to drop things on the bottom of the boat as the sound will reverberate through the water and scare them away.' She also remembered her father catching fish. 'Dad got a massive eighteen-pounder once. I tried to reel it in but couldn't hold it.'

A gentle tug at her hook had her sitting up straight. 'Come on, take the bait.'

'You got one?'

Sienna grinned. 'I might have,' she teased, though it was only an inquisitive fish checking out what was on offer.

Harry was working from the other side of the boat. 'More than I've had so far.'

Sunscreen was smeared roughly on his face and arms while a wide-brimmed hat shadowed his cheeks. Knots formed in her stomach. This was the life. A day on the briny with someone she cared about. Now all they needed was a big, fat snapper.

An hour and a half later Sienna landed her

second brim of the day. The fish had finally started biting in earnest on the turn of the tide, resulting in Harry having three in the chilly bin already.

'Not the big snapper everyone wants to catch, but young ones are juicier,' she said, now remembering catching a fish with her father. Those were his exact words. 'Thank you for bringing me here. I'm having fun.' The past and the present were melding, bringing together both her lives, making her feel a little bit more whole than she had done since she'd become an adult in charge of her life. All because of this man. Which meant he had the power to wreck it too. She shuddered.

'So you're glad I dragged you out of bed early?'

'There wasn't much dragging going on.' And that was what she had to hold on to now, not spend precious time thinking about what could go wrong. 'But if you'd thrown me over your shoulder and taken me away then, well, we mightn't have made it to Coromandel.' Not until they'd had time in his bed first.

Harry grinned. 'Let's head in. We've got more than enough fish for dinner, and I'd like to go for a drive over the other side of the peninsula, mosey around some.'

'Sounds perfect.' More time getting to know Harry better, and better. The more she learned about him, the more she had to know. It was as though she had an insatiable appetite for all things Harry.

They moseyed and talked, drank a beer at a pub and talked, before Harry suggested they head back to their accommodation.

'I can run with that. In fact, I'm salivating about barbecued fish with fresh bread for dinner.'

'I'm disappointed.'

'Oh, all right, I'll dribble about testing out that bed again before the fish.' It wouldn't be hard to delay a meal for making love. There was hunger to appease her stomach, and then there was downright hungry for Harrison. No contest.

Later that night, Sienna fell into the deepest sleep the moment her head hit the pillow, only to wake when Harry wound his arm around her and snuggled into her back. Of course, she wasn't going to miss out on any touching time.

Touching which progressed so that they weren't lying quietly for long.

'What made you want to become a doctor?' Harry asked when their heart rates were back to normal and their bodies languishing in after-match stupor.

Where did that come from? Sienna wondered. 'When I was eleven I had an appendectomy and according to my dad I didn't stop asking questions about why an appendix could get infected, what would happen if it wasn't removed, why it had happened to me. I know I wasn't satisfied with some of the answers nurses fobbed me off with, so when I got home I tried to find out everything I could. I was becoming a science nerd.'

'That was enough to make you want to do medicine?'

'Not at all. The nurses were kind and did everything to make me feel better—apart from answer my questions—and I planned on being a nurse when I grew up.'

'But that science nerd took over?' Harry's fingers were making soft circles on her skin.

'Yes, thank goodness. I can't think of being anything else.'

'Why paediatrics?'

Ah.

'I've always liked kids, especially the little ones with their inquisitive minds and willing-ness to try out anything before they learn they might get hurt or make a mistake.'

And I was never sure if I'd be lucky enough to have my own family.

'What made you take up emergency medi-cine? Apart from being an adrenalin junkie,' she asked.

'Not so much the adrenalin rush as the need for action, the urgency, putting things to rights as soon as possible. Not that I always save my patients, but I put everything on the line in the attempt.'

'How's that related to your past?'

'Don't hold back, will you?' Those fingers didn't hesitate with their circles.

'Sometimes it's the only way to find out what I want.'

They lay there for a while and Sienna knew he wasn't going to answer her. Disappointing as that was, she accepted his choice. They might be getting along better than ever but, since it wasn't a permanent thing, he didn't owe her details of his past. Unfortunately.

Then his hand stopped, his fingers splaying across her waist, holding her lightly, as if he was acknowledging they were together, however temporarily. 'As an emergency doc, I go in, do all I can to fix up a patient and discharge them, or get them stable to move on to a specialist ward where they'll get the care they need, and I move on to the next person needing immediate attention. In and out. Done and dusted. It works for me.'

'None of the long-term involvement.' Like his relationships with women by the sound of things. Like his connection with his parents. Short and sharp. Was everyone the result of their childhood? Their adolescence?

'Yeah,' he sighed, and his fingers went back to making those relaxing circles on her skin, making her sleepy again.

As Sienna drifted into sleep Harry stared at the darkened ceiling, trying not to admit the day had been one of the greatest he'd known in a very long time—if not the best ever. They'd been so comfortable together it was as though they'd known each other for a lot longer than a few weeks. Yet they knew next to nothing really, not the deep, hurtful reasons for being who they'd become. Sure, there'd been some give and take about family and growing up, but they'd only scratched the surface, yet still this felt different, like a real friendship. Friendship with benefits? No. A true, deep and meaningful relationship had to have it all. Was it possible that Sienna would give him that and more? Had they found a connection because they were both marked by their pasts? Did the reason even matter?

She flung an arm out, clobbered him lightly on the chest and muttered incoherently before settling further into her pillow.

He waited, breathing deep the scent that was Sienna. And knew hope. Knew they were special together. Knew this fling would still have to run its course because he wasn't prepared to take a risk again.

Sunday brought more of the same: sex, a leisurely breakfast, fishing... Except instead of driving along the coast to visit other towns, the excursion drew to a finish. Reluctantly Sienna climbed into the four-wheel drive, sensing that more than the weekend was over. If not today, then soon. In one sense she felt happier than she had in a long time, in another way she'd been given a taste of something that was not long-term. 'That was fabulous. Thank you so much for taking me along.'

'It wouldn't have been half the fun on my own.' Then Harry gulped and went all silent on her. Realising he did like sharing his time with someone? With her, even?

She wasn't asking. The answer might be confronting and that was not how she wanted to end this interlude. While the kilometres ticked over and the Coromandel Peninsula disappeared behind them before the Bombay Hills on the outskirts of Auckland began to fill their vision, she refused to dwell on anything but how enjoyable these two days had been, not on what she'd been missing out on. Finally she told Harry, 'I'd forgotten how much fun doing something simple like fishing could be. Dad and I used to go out quite a lot in some places we stayed.'

'You'd do it again?'

'With you?' She winced. Wrong thing to say.

'Yes, if the opportunity arose, but then it's not likely to, is it?'

'I can't imagine I'll get another chance before I head away.' Definitely reminding her he wasn't here for ever.

Then slam. Out of nowhere it hit hard.

I am like Dad. I do enjoy wandering about with no timetable to adhere to.

Putting emphasis on keeping her life orderly all her adult life was designed to make her feel normal. Other people went fishing, played sports or partied, had lots of friends around them, and stayed in one place. This past week had opened her eyes, and she'd hardly started on that list. All she had to do was find a balance between who she needed to be and the girl who wanted to toss caution to the wind and have a ball every day. It did not have to mean reverting to the girl child on the road. Yeah, sure. 'I've been fooling myself all along.' A shiver rattled down her spine.

'What are you talking about?'

She'd said that out loud? See, already losing control. 'Nothing.'

'Sienna? What's going on?'

'Nothing,' she repeated. When had she become such a fool? It had taken nothing more than a wonderful weekend to loosen all the restraints she'd spent her adult life putting in place.

'You're shutting down on me.'

How could he think that? 'No, I'm not. Because of this weekend I'm starting to understand all that I've been missing out on, and that I can't let go entirely if I don't want to be like my father.'

Harry clenched the steering wheel. This couldn't happen. Sienna needed to live life to the full. She'd missed out on too much already, and he didn't want to be the one who showed how it could be if she wasn't going to follow through. That'd make him feel guilty, like waving chocolate in front of her then eating it himself. 'You've got another week's leave yet. Plenty more time to catch up on some of those things you want to do.' He also wanted this Sienna to become stronger. They'd got on so well he'd miss her if she reverted to her old self.

Like you're hanging around to notice?

His heart dived to his toes. No, but he could

get something from knowing she was succeeding with moving on.

Not good enough, Harry.

It was the best he could come up with right now. He was not putting his heart on the line again, even if it had taken a hit these past couple of days. 'There's nothing to stop you carrying on with your list.'

Her gaze was fixed on something beyond the front of the car. 'I hope you're right. I've had a blast this weekend. But it's also brought back memories of a past I've strived hard to keep under lockdown.' Her finger was picking at the hem of her denim shorts above her knee.

'You're frightened?'

'What if I can't get myself back under control?'

'Would that be a bad thing if it's what you truly want?' What was an out-of-control-out-of-bed Sienna truly like? Exciting? Enchanting? Infuriating? Guess he'd never know.

I'd like to know.

Again, his heart did a dive. Again, he ignored it.

'I might not know where to stop. My father has never let me forget the time I said I wanted to take to the air and swoop over the world observing everyone and everything. It was a child's fantasy that had nothing to do with real life.' Pick, pick. There'd be no hem left if she continued.

But Harry kept on his own scratching. 'Do you really want to live in a way that doesn't make you happy?' He needed to know this. It would explain Sienna better.

Sienna swallowed hard. Why was Harry pushing her? It wasn't as if he'd done much more at sorting out *his* life. 'Being a doctor is more important to me than going off for a day on a boat or driving to another town for a week.' So was finding the love of her life and settling down to raise a family with him, but that was definitely under lock and key. Not going on the list. Her eyes slid sideways. No, Harrison was adorable, too easy to fall in love with—if she hadn't already. He *was* the man she'd like in her life for ever, but he wasn't available because of his own issues. Going there would be too frightening. But equally tempting.

'You've been happy these past few days. Keep pushing yourself, Sienna.'

'You're great at handing out advice, aren't you? Tried following any yourself?'

'Yeah,' he drawled. 'I took you away for the weekend.'

'You enjoyed it?'

'You have to ask?'

Sienna shook her head. 'No, I don't. But that frightens you. You're as messed up as me.' But nor did she want to stop being with him, while Harry might walk away from her when they got home. Which was moments away.

Harrison nodded. 'True, but there again, we went into this knowing there's a cut-off point, and to make the most of our time together.'

That was what was starting to frighten her. D-day. If she didn't want to stop seeing him now, how would she feel in a couple of weeks? Would her heart withstand the pain of letting him go? There were risks involved with living a well-rounded life.

Turning into his drive, Harry told her, 'I'll unpack and prepare some of that fish for dinner.'

'Sure. I'll take my bag home and grab some wine.' She eased out of the four-wheel drive and, hands on hips, stretched up on her toes to relieve the tightness in her back from the ride, while ignoring the bands of worry in her head. Enjoy the moment, seize the night.

Minutes later she walked around the corner of Harry's apartment and heard him saying, 'When's the start date?'

She paused, her heart nearly deafening her.

But not enough. Harry was saying, 'That'd work in perfectly with me finishing here at Christmas. I said I'd never return to Melbourne, but there's nothing else out there at the moment, and I need to leave Auckland.'

Sienna closed her eyes, trying to block out those words. Too late. They were pummelling her from inside her skull. He *had* to leave Auckland. Because of her?

Harry hadn't finished. 'It might be time I gave the old city a try.' A pause, obviously listening to his caller. Then, 'You know if I say I'll take it on I'll see it through.'

Wake-up call, Si. Harry's moving on.

He'd never led her to believe differently, but hearing it for real hurt, and proved she'd been living in la-la land for the past few days. But what days they had been. The best. Couldn't complain about that. Would she do it all over if she'd heard this phone call beforehand? Yes. Without a doubt. Harry had been good for her. Could be better, but that wasn't going to happen.

'Okay, Lance, I'll give you a call after I've read the contract. I'd have done it earlier but I've been busy. See you.'

Busy. With her. Like she'd been a mission now completed. Two could play that game, and save her heart along the way.

Go home and tick off the fling early. Try not to let this get to you.

There were always going to be knock-backs but this was the one she really, really didn't want, even when she'd known it was coming.

At Harrison's back door she paused, drank in the sight of him as he put down his phone and began on the fish. Dressed in his knee-length shorts and a tee shirt that hugged his pecs, he was every inch the man of her dreams. How was she going to turn her back on him now that she knew every part of that body, the pleasure he gave? He took?

Harry looked up from the plates he'd filled with flour, breadcrumbs and a bowl with egg to coat the fish. 'Come in and pour yourself a glass.'

Suddenly her appetite for food fled, leaving her sagging—yet still hungry for Harrison. She could stay for another night of wonderment, or she could go while she was able. 'I'll forgo dinner, thanks.'

'There's plenty of time tomorrow to do whatever's bothering you.' His words were straightforward, but the shutters were coming down in his eyes. He knew she was pulling out early. 'Don't end a great weekend this way.'

'Sorry, Harrison, I really am, but it's how it is.'

Turn around and walk. Now. Don't step closer to him...don't reach out to touch him.

Jerking about, she carefully trod down the steps and onto the path that'd take her back home to safety and control. Every time her foot moved forward she fought not to spin around and rush into his arms.

'Si,' Harry called softly, then said no more.

Sienna was relieved. There wasn't anything he could say. They were always going to break up, it had just come about quicker and sharper than expected. Hearing him discuss his next job was a timely reminder. She had to look out for her heart. She paused to draw a breath. But she'd continue her leave this coming week and start learning the intricacies of flying. It was time to find the middle road for her future. It mightn't end up being perfect, the man she might've begun falling in love with wouldn't be there to share it, but there would be more than medicine to keep her going. So sensible. So darned awful. Lonely. Heart breaking, if that cracking, aching sensation already going on in her chest was an indicator.

Back inside her apartment Sienna wandered through to the lounge and studied the Christmas tree. Her fingers itched to tidy it up, balance the decorations, make it all perfect—make her life perfect again. Turning her back on it, she went to poach an egg for dinner. Having no appetite didn't mean not eating.

Silence weighed down on her. The weekend had been full of laughter and chatter. She and Harrison saw eye to eye on many things, and argued like stink on plenty of others. That was one of the best things about their relationship. Huh? Before the mind-zapping, body-melting sex? Yes. No. Oh, whatever. It had all been magic, and now it wasn't. There was a quick fix—go back over the way and apologise and enjoy being with Harry until he left at Christmas. And *then* go through this indecision and pain.

It hurt now. It would only get worse if she made love to Harrison for days and nights all the while knowing she was snatching at moments. He was leaving Auckland. Putting distance between them. Guess it was better than him staying here where she ran the risk of bumping into him through work.

Under the hot shower she rested her head against the glass wall and let the warmth relax the tension in her back, her arms and legs. Unfortunately, the heat did nothing for her heavy heart and the sadness swamping her mind. This was reality. It was over with Harrison. Overhearing that phone call had been the catalyst to protect herself, making her understand that a fling wasn't done in isolation. It involved head and heart, new needs and longings she hadn't known before and didn't want to let go; and afterwards none of the emotions could be switched off with a single flick.

The coming days with him right next door were going to be difficult. Painful. Filled with temptation to rush across and pick up where she'd left off.

But I will get through them. I have to. Please.

Starting with ignoring the dull thud going on behind her ribs, constantly reminding her of what she was walking away from.

CHAPTER TEN

'HARRY...'

Sienna's sweet voice broke through the clouds in his head.

Timing was everything, apparently. He could've checked the mailbox ten minutes ago, instead of sitting staring at his feet thinking of what might've been with Sienna if he had the guts to give it a go. He could've prepped the steak he'd bought for dinner before he came out here. By then surely she'd have gone inside. 'Hey, there. How's things?' His hands gripped his hips. It wasn't that he didn't want to see her, more that he already knew the pain that would follow as he watched her walk back up to her apartment alone.

Sienna swung around the end of her drive, a large smile splitting her face. 'You've got to see this.'

He did? What was so important she wanted him to take a look? It could be her report card from primary school and he'd willingly read it. 'What've you got?'

'My very own pilot's logbook.' She skidded to a halt in front of him and opened to the first page. 'See, those are my hours, and that shows what the lesson was about, and that's the type of plane.'

'Whoa, that's awesome. You've done one-hour-five in total over two days?'

'The lessons are intense and, therefore, not very long at first. But, Harry, it was fantastic. I'm learning climbing and descending.' Her hand rose and fell in gentle waves. 'Tomorrow I'm starting on turns.'

'Who'd have thought you could get so excited about making a turn?' His laugh was low and a little sad. Had she been excited when she did an about-face on him?

'I know.' She snapped the book shut. 'Sorry, I got a bit carried away.' Stepping away, she drew her shoulders back, determination now covering her beautiful face. 'How're things with you?' Determined to be polite, not excited and happy?

That hurt. He didn't deserve it. They had both agreed to a fling, not for ever after. He just hadn't been ready for the finish, was all. Was still getting used to it. 'I've left a chilly bin by your back door with some fish fillets on ice. You might want to eat them tonight or put them in the freezer.' He began to walk away, unable to stand there and not haul her into his arms and kiss the daylights out of them both. Yeah, he still wanted her. And that was something that had never happened before, not in a long time at any rate.

'Thanks.' Then, 'Harry, are you all right? Why aren't you at work?' She sounded concerned.

Unfortunately he couldn't use it to his advantage. 'I'm fine. Got today and tomorrow off as I'm working the weekend.'

'I'm glad nothing's wrong.'

Oh, believe me, plenty's wrong.

How to fix it was another story. He stomped up the drive and inside to unpack groceries, open every window in the place, hang out the washing. Oil and season the steak. Mundane, meant to distract the picture of Sienna seared at the front of his brain, and not working. Now what? He'd been on the go since six and it was only ten and he didn't know how to fill in the rest of the day. This was when living in a town where he didn't know anyone other than colleagues sucked. No one to ring and say 'Want to go for a run, or a beer, or a game of squash?' At least returning to Melbourne would change that, if nothing else.

No point looking over the fence. Sienna had gone out again, probably headed to the aero club and another lesson that got her all wound up in a ball of barely contained excitement. He'd never seen her so happy. Or maybe he had when they made love, or when she'd caught her first fish the other day. Long may it last. She deserved it. If only he could find the tenacity to hang around and share her happiness. Harry shivered. This wasn't about doggedness. It was about risk-taking, and where his heart was concerned that wasn't happening.

So he needed to find something to fill in his time.

The lawns could do with a cut. He got a sweat up fast in the heat. It felt good, worked some of the hurt out of his system. Hurt he shouldn't be feeling. They'd had a fling, and now Sienna had beat him to pulling the plug. If he'd done it. The weekend in Coromandel had shown him another side to Sienna, and to himself. It had woken up those old dreams of love and family and settling in one place.

His legs ate up the lawn as he raced round and round. The middle came way too fast. He needed to expend more energy. Sienna's lawns could do with a cut. She wouldn't thank him. Too bad. He didn't need thanks. Just a kiss.

No, not a kiss, you idiot.

She could ignore him for all he cared. But he would mow the lawn for her.

Round and round and round until he reached the centre.

She'd go ape—no straight lines to be seen, but there was nothing she could do about it, just as there was nothing he could do about her calling off their fling before he was ready.

Now he'd earned a beer. But who to call? Everyone was at work. Except his neighbour, and he was not calling her. Grabbing a glass of icy water, he went to find his laptop and cruised the medical sites for jobs that didn't involve Melbourne, and his parents, and all the things he'd spent years avoiding. More importantly, he had to find one that wasn't in Auckland, because he needed to avoid Sienna more than anything.

She'd pressed some buttons, kick starting emotions that he didn't want to admit to. So he'd go for broke and do his usual—he'd move on.

On Wednesday afternoon Sienna indicated to turn into her driveway but the old man in the wheelchair kept on going right into her path. 'Watch out.'

Clunk. The wheelchair bounced off her bumper, teetered on one wheel before banging down on the other and rolling on down the road.

'What?' She quickly pulled into her driveway and hauled the brake on before leaping out and running after the man.

He was out of control and heading into the path of another oncoming car. 'Stop,' she shouted. 'Look out.'

The driver of the car couldn't hear her with her windows closed, and if the old man had he didn't understand or was incapable of acting on it. She ran, her breath stuck in her throat as she waited for the inevitable, and hoped impact wouldn't be too nasty.

It was worse. The chair slammed square on the front grill and the man was tossed out and under the engine.

The car wheels squealed as brakes were applied, then the driver screamed. 'What happened? Where did you come from?'

Sienna reached them. 'Turn off the motor while I check out how the man's situated under there.'

'Shouldn't I back off?'

'No,' she all but shouted. 'The gentleman might be caught on a part of your car and we don't want you dragging him along the road.'

The woman blanched. 'Just as well you're thinking straight. I'd have injured him even more.'

Deep breath as she kneeled down. 'It's all right. We've got this.'

'Is he caught in the wheelchair?' came a familiar voice.

'He's strapped in,' she told Harrison as she took in the odd angle of the man's arm and the blood pouring from the side of his head. And the lax mouth. 'I wonder if he had a medical event. He wasn't controlling the wheelchair at all.'

'I heard a bang and came rushing out to see what had happened.' Harry lowered onto his stomach and pushed forward, his head disappearing under the car, still talking. 'Did he hit your car first?'

'Bounced off the bumper.' She squatted beside Harry and looked at how to disentangle their man. 'This isn't going to be easy.'

Wriggling out, Harry stood up and pulled his phone out. 'I'll call 111 and then get my medical bag. Do you have one in your apartment?'

Shaking her head, she admitted, 'Only the basic bandages and creams.'

'Our man needs a lot more than that.' Harry rattled off details and the address to the emergency service.

Sienna straightened up. 'I'll get your gear. Emergencies are more your strength.' She could do what was required, but why not give the old man the best chance they had available and right now that was Harrison?

'See if there's a crowbar in the garage, would you? I'd like to shift this bumper off his chest if I can.'

'On my way.' Ducking inside the apartment, she retrieved the medical kit before heading into the garage to search through the biggest collection of tools she'd ever encountered. Everything but a crowbar. Would a hammer be large enough? Snatching the largest one, she spun around to head outside and stopped. A crowbar hung from a nail on the far wall, half-hidden by a raincoat. 'Yeah.'

Back beside Harry she opened the kit so he could get at anything he needed. Then she began checking over the man's legs, searching for broken bones.

'I think he's had a stroke,' Harry said quietly.

'That would explain the loss of control over the wheelchair.' At least he was still breathing. 'Lack of consciousness?'

'There's an impact injury to the skull, but the stroke might've caused him to lose full consciousness before. Did you notice anything out of the ordinary?' Harry was working at stemming the bleeding.

'Only that he didn't seem to see my car, nor hear me when I yelled to watch out.' Shuffling closer, she put her hand over Harry's where he pressed against the wound. 'Let me do that while you try and shift the bumper.'

Harrison handed over immediately and studied the bent and buckled wheelchair. 'It's stuck hard. We've got the fire service coming. Those guys will have cutting equipment. I doubt the crowbar will be of any use without hurting our man further.'

'There's a siren now,' a woman said in a trembling voice.

Sienna glanced up to see the driver of the car watching them worriedly. 'You okay?'

'Not really. I could've killed him.'

'He is alive, but we think he's had a stroke, so don't go blaming yourself.' She turned back to their patient and with her free hand began checking his pulse again.

'Can you move left a bit?' Harry asked as he bent back some broken wheel spokes.

'Sure.' Working alongside Harrison felt right. They just clicked. As they did with most things. Except her lawn. Even in her new, slightly relaxed state, those circles drove her nuts. 'Thanks for mowing the lawn, by the way.'

He didn't look her way, so focused was he on the bolt he was trying to undo, but his grin was obvious. 'No problem.'

She wouldn't give him the satisfaction of knowing he'd annoyed her. If he hadn't already guessed. Plastering on a big smile in case he looked her way, she continued checking her patient.

Her smile faltered. She dragged it back in place. Harrison was a problem, but that didn't mean everything else was stalled. By starting to do things outside work she might become better prepared for a man in her future, whether it was Harrison or not. In her chest her heart slowed, unhappy about the idea of any man other than Harry. Okay, it seemed Harrison owned her heart. But for now she had to concentrate on getting her act together, becoming a rounded person with more to her bow than medicine.

If she had to pretend to be happy, then she'd keep pretending until it became real.

'Harry, got a minute?' the base director called as he made his way out of the changing room, dressed in light shorts and an even lighter shirt, the Santa suit he'd started wearing this week hanging on the peg for tomorrow. Seemed the kids loved Father Christmas turning up to save them.

That blasted humidity was doing a number on Harry again. 'Sure, Derek.' It was Friday night and he'd prefer a cold beer with the crew than what was probably going to be a discussion about how he thought the past three months had gone for him.

A chilled wine with a certain lady as company would be even better.

Yeah, well, that was not happening. Wine hadn't been his favourite drink until a little over a week ago and he needed to move past that. The door had slammed shut on that particular relationship.

Sienna was busy getting on with her life and he was still in his nice, comfortable holding pattern of work, drinks with the crew, and avoiding everything else. Except the more he saw Sienna going out or arriving home well after him, the angrier he got with himself. Doing the same old same old wasn't working any more. He wanted more, wanted to partake in living, not remain on the sidelines. In other words, he wanted to watch trees grow. Just as Sienna was doing. If she could sort herself out, surely he could manage the same?

'Take a load off.' Derek nodded to the chair on the opposite side of his desk and handed across his dream libation.

'You read my mind.' Hopefully only about the beer.

'It's stinking hot and we're both off duty, so why not? This will hardly touch the sides.'

Harry poured beer into his mouth, savoured the chill, the flavour, then swallowed. 'You softening me up for extra shifts?' Some of the medical staff were trying to get days off for Christmas shopping and other pre-season stuff that needed doing before hordes of family descended upon them. He didn't have that problem.

'There is that, but what I want to ask is— what are your plans once you're finished with us? Have you got another contract lined up?'

'Sort of. I haven't dotted the i's and crossed the t's but there's a contract in my inbox.' It needed signing and returning, fast. The days in Auckland were running out and he didn't want to be left languishing. Definitely not in Auckland, where there was every chance of bumping into Sienna. Time to put this little glitch behind him and pull his finger out. He had to or go spare with need. He had to get away. Siberia wasn't quite on the cards, but desperation did strange things to a man. 'I've been offered the HOD's position at Melbourne General for a year.'

The man opposite him nodded. 'That sounds too good to turn down.'

'It is, but for personal reasons I'm hedging my bets.' Which wasn't fair on Lance. He'd get on to that the moment he got home tonight.

'Then you might be interested in staying on in Auckland. Working with us,' he added quickly.

He'd walked into that one, hadn't he? Too busy thinking about Sienna. 'I'm not interested in continuing to live here either.' But even as the words formed he was weighing up everything for and against. Getting away from being next door to Sienna was right up there, but there were other apartments or flats in this city that he could rent. On the plus side it meant not returning to Melbourne. Harry continued. 'Tell me more about this position. How long do you need someone? What's the role?'

'This is confidential, you understand.'

'You have my word.'

'I'm going to Europe indefinitely with my wife. She's Italian and wants to spend time with her relatives over there. There're also lots of other countries we'd like to visit for more than a day or two crowded amongst millions of tourists, which is possible if we're there out of peak season.'

'Sounds fantastic.' Harry drained his bottle. That sort of trip wasn't something he'd do but then he didn't have anyone to share the experience with, so he'd never given it much thought. It wouldn't be half as enjoyable doing it alone.

Do you want to travel, Sienna?

The beer choked him. Wiping his mouth with the back of his hand, he stared at his white knuckles. He'd got it bad. Perhaps he should go abroad, work in faraway places, and get over what ailed him.

Derek got two more beers from the small fridge shunted into a corner out of the way of medical packs and equipment. As he handed over a bottle he looked around his cramped office and then outside to where the helicopters were parked. 'This would be a permanent position.'

'Has this been approved by the board?' There was no way the base director could make the offer off his own bat. The board would want a say in the matter—*all* the say.

'They know and have agreed for me to approach you. You've impressed everyone with your cool, calm way of approaching patients and staff alike. If you don't want to accept then we'll have to go through the laborious process of advertising.'

'Laying it on thick, aren't you?' Harry chuckled.

'Of course. Tell me you're not a little bit interested.'

The guy was good at this. 'You already know the answer to that. I am thoroughly enjoying working here.'

'But you're not so keen on our great city.'

'A city is a city.' *Saying too much, Harry.*

'So there's someone in this particular city you want to avoid? Don't you know the population is well over a million and a half?'

Yes, he did, but there were only so many hospitals and paediatric wards to go round, and in this job he visited all of them one week or another. 'I'm not going to give you an answer today.'

'Fair enough. That's better than I'd expected after you said you wanted to get away. But don't take too long, eh?'

'I can shake on that.'

'No need. Your word's good enough for me.'

Derek shoved his chair back and stood up. 'Feel up to a couple more beers at my place along with a barbecue and meeting Lisa?'

He knew when he was being set up. All part of the conditioning process, and no one could blame this man for trying. 'I'd like that.'

'Good. Hans and his wife will be there too.' As in board-member Hans.

Too late to pull out—if he wanted to, and right this moment he wasn't sure. Something about staying on in this particular service, this city, was pulling at him. Something he suspected revolved entirely around Sienna and what they'd started. She might've finished it but his heart still had to catch up, let her go. Or dive in deep. He shivered. 'No problem.' He'd buy a bottle of wine for Lisa on the way. Which promptly reminded him of the last bottle he'd bought and who for. Which in turn underscored exactly why he had to say no to this opportunity. Or did he?

Sienna would tell him where to stick that thought if she knew. She'd feed him back his own line about avoiding life. Damn, but they were alike, yet acting out their lives in opposite directions. Or had been until she cycled off that hill. The thought of signing on for a position with no end date in sight no longer frightened him as much as it once had. Getting old? At thirty-six? He grunted a sour laugh. No, but this constant moving around was getting old. The idea of waking up to the same possessions around him, the same people every day, the same town or city, was starting to become a persistent nag in the back of his head.

I planted trees I want to see grow.

Sienna. Of course. Damn her.

Get out of my head, will you?

'I need wine.' A glance at her phone told Sienna it was well after nine. Hardly wine o'clock. Too bad. Her last glass of wine had been on the lawn of the bach in Coromandel, with Harry beside her telling some embellished story about a road trip he'd done in outback Australia. She'd poured one the first night home after the weekend, and ended up tipping it out, unable to face it on her own. Wine was for enjoyment, for sharing, for laughter and chatter.

And for celebrating spreading my wings. Tick.

There was a bottle of champagne in the back

of the fridge, put there yonks ago when a grateful parent had given it to her for saving his daughter's life. Normally gifts from patients and parents went into the staff pool, but Dale had insisted she take this one home—the patient had been his niece. The bottle had languished in the fridge waiting for the right occasion. Well, tonight she'd finally found one.

The sound of the plastic cork popping made her smile, but as she poured the liquid into her glass the smile drooped. Champagne wasn't made for drinking alone. New life, remember? The list was making things happen. Celebrate.

A vehicle pulled into the drive next door, making her pause. Harry was late home. Friday-night drinks with the crews? But his arrival was perfect timing if she had the courage to invite him in for a drink. He'd say no. She'd apologise for everything she'd said. He'd still say no. Did she need that?

Yes, if she was going to keep moving forward. No, because rejection stung.

'Harry,' she called over the fence. 'I've just opened a bottle of champagne. Would you like a glass?' He was probably thinking she had an alcohol problem, given the time of night.

His head appeared around the back of his four-wheel drive. 'I've already had a couple of beers.'

'Fair enough.' She turned away. At least she'd tried.

Call that trying? Come on, Si.

Turning back, she drew a shaky breath. 'I'm celebrating a grand total of three hours ten minutes' flying time.' Nerves warred with jubilation. 'I don't really like drinking alone.'

His sigh was loud enough to be heard across the fence. 'Pour me a glass. I'll be right over.'

She headed inside so she couldn't hear when he called out his change of mind. Champagne spilled over the bench as she tried to fill a glass for him.

'So you're still getting a buzz out of heading up into the sky in a tiny flying machine?'

Sienna whirled around to stare at him standing in her doorway. 'Absolutely. I should have done it ages ago. Right from the first time rolling down the runway it's been thrilling. Very different to anything I've ever done before. Exciting, scary, demanding.' Slow down. Harrison could still disappear on her if he thought she'd lost her mind.

He stepped inside. 'So your fear of heights hasn't raised its head as the hours go up?'

Handing him the glass with champagne inside and on the outside, she stared at him. Wow, he was gorgeous, but she already knew that. Now that she'd experienced his lovemaking there was no going back on her feelings for him. All she could do was rein them in while he was close. 'Not one moment of trepidation.'

'So no jumping off a building needed.' That couldn't be disappointment in his voice, surely?

The bungee-jumping idea still rattled her. 'No.' Not even with you.

'I'm impressed.' Harrison moved across to the table and pulled out two chairs, tilting his head at one.

Sinking onto the seat, she sipped her drink, needing the false sense of courage it gave her. If only he'd smile at her, turn her insides to mush. Then what? They had fallen out; he was here out of politeness, not because he wanted to make love with her.

'Thanks, so am I. I haven't been scared once. Honestly, when I hold the controls and the instructor tells me to pull back slowly and steadily and the nose of the plane comes up and then we're off the ground and the plane's flying because I did that—along with a lot of help—it's the most incredible sensation out there. I can't get enough of it.'

A bit like you. I can't get enough of you, and yet there are times when I want nothing to do with you.

Harry sat, stretching his legs half across the dining room. 'Go you. What's next? Going onto the bridge of a cruise ship and taking that out to sea?'

He'd seen her list, knew everything that was on it. Including having a fling. Tick. She hadn't written 'end the fling quickly' but mentally she gave that a tick too. 'I might plan a short trip to South America to see Dad some time in the new year.' Since when? Since right this moment. It wasn't her preferred option but it was a load better than not continuing to push the boundaries. 'I'm getting the hang of this.' Hopefully not so much that she turned into a clone of her father.

'You won't want to return to the ward.'

His ability to read her mind still flummoxed her. 'Yes, I will. I'll always be a doctor at heart. That's who I am before anything else.' The wine was top-of-the-range yet she wasn't getting the buzz she'd expected.

'So you'll start using up some of the leave you've got accruing.' He swirled the champagne around in his glass, staring into it as if he was looking for something. But all he said was, 'Are you heading back to work on Monday?'

'Yes. The body's back to normal, no aches or bruises.' Though sometimes if she moved suddenly her ribs would give her grief.

Harrison's eyes widened when she said body, but he didn't give her the once-over. There certainly wasn't any lust going on in his expression. He had got over her—very fast. 'That's good. I saw you coming back from a ride last night. The new bike looks like it's got every bell and whistle going.'

Had he been looking out for her? Can't have. He was giving off vibes that said he wanted nothing more to do with her. 'I upgraded.' Damn this. 'What have you been doing since the weekend other than work?'

His shrug was eloquent, and really annoying. 'Not a lot. The job takes most of my time, as you know.'

'Sure. But there's more to life than work,' she gave back, tired of being the only one who had to sort out her life. 'You could find a permanent job somewhere and stop running away.'

Rolling his glass back and forth between his hands, he glared at her. 'You don't pull any punches, do you?'

Her chin jutted forward. 'I'm learning. And guess who taught me?'

The glare faded, replaced with something like longing. 'Glad I've been some use.'

'Some use?' Harrison hadn't pushed her off the road that night, though he had distracted her enough to lose concentration, but he hadn't let her get away with her need to keep everything under control either. 'That accident woke me up to certain things.' Be honest, if nothing else. 'But your irritating habit of rubbing me up the wrong way has helped. A lot.'

His eyes widened again, and his fingers relaxed their dangerous grip on the glass. 'Even when you didn't agree?'

'Mostly when I didn't agree with your damned fool suggestions.'

'None of them were foolish, just backing up what you really wanted to do in the first place.'

Man, he could be such a know-it-all.

'You—'

No, stop.

Playing *You said... I said; if I can do this, you can too* wasn't going to get her anywhere. He was going to head back over the fence shortly, leaving her to her sad heart.

'This is crazy.' Draining her glass, she reached for the bottle. 'More?'

He'd barely started the first glassful. 'No.' The glass started twirling between his fingers again.

Silence fell between them.

Sienna sipped her wine, trying to enjoy it. This was a celebration, after all. Not that anyone was dancing or singing.

'I got a job offer today.'

Great. Not. No denying he was leaving now. Melbourne here he comes. 'When do you start?'

'I haven't said yes.'

He'd been cagey the night she'd overheard his side of the conversation. Might as well pretend she knew nothing about that. 'Is it too close to your current one?' As in, right here, staying in the apartment next door and having to see her most days of the week, close?

'It is my current one.' Now he emptied his glass in one long swallow.

That got her attention. 'Seriously?' Definitely as in right here, staying in the apartment next door and having to see her most days of the week, close. Her heart whacked out of rhythm, unable to absorb this news.

'As I told you, I haven't said yes yet.'

He didn't have to sound so down about it. Sienna pushed the bottle across. 'So my neighbours aren't returning?' She wanted to be excited at the chance Harry might be next door for a while to come, but how could she be when the dark expression on his face told her it was the last thing he wanted? She might love him, but she didn't want him at any cost. He had to feel the same about her and obviously that wasn't the case. Had never been.

'Okay, not quite the same job. Yes, your neighbours are returning, but the base director is leaving and his job's mine if I want it.' The darkness was still there in his eyes, his mouth tight, his cheeks pale.

'You're not exactly leaping in the air with excitement so I'd suggest you turn it down.' How she managed to get those words out was beyond her, but they had to be said, and in the long run this was about protecting herself. Draining her glass, she struggled to swallow the now less than wonderful liquid for the lump in her throat.

Don't let him ruin your day.

With grim determination she refilled both glasses and raised hers to tap the rim against Harry's. 'Here's to making the right decision.'

He didn't return the tap. 'How does anyone know they've got it right? You hear so often about people at crossroads and selecting one way when it turns out the other would've been best.'

'Or worse.' This time it was easier to swallow. 'Like you've told me, don't let the past hold you back. Work out what you want and go for it, boots and all.'

'Where do you want to be in six months' time?' There was genuine interest in his eyes and face, and his voice had lightened from that dark huskiness.

Living with you.

But that wasn't something she could share. It was so new and raw, so fragile, she could break if he didn't treat her with care. And he had no reason to. She only had herself to blame for falling for him. 'It's still a work in progress.'

His face shut down, and he stood up, setting his glass aside. 'Time I headed away. It's been a long day.'

The fingers holding the stem of her glass whitened. 'Sure. Good luck with the decision about the job.'

'Yeah, it isn't easy.' He stood looking down at her, something very like need in his gaze, making her heart whack harder. But then he took a step away. And another, aiming for her back door. 'Thanks for the drink.'

The door closed behind him with a soft click. He was gone. Again.

No way would Harrison take up the offer of a permanent position with the rescue service. 'He's just like my dad.' Gulping a mouthful of champagne didn't ease the pain, even as bubbles tingled on her tongue. 'Never stopping in one place long enough to make friends.' This had been a celebration that had turned to mud, but she wasn't giving up. After pouring the last of the wine into her glass she leaned back on her chair and stared at the door, hearing that click over and over. Harrison had gone.

She'd been the one to leave him on Sunday, and the result was the same. It hurt beyond what she'd ever known. Worse than when her parents broke up and her dad left for good. This was closer, was her pain. It broke her heart, that was what it did. Smashed it to smithereens, and there wasn't a glue in the world that could hold it together now. 'I want to follow you to the end of the earth, Harry, but I can't. I would destroy both of us, living your way of life. It's in me to move around non-stop and yet I hate doing it, hate the consequences. So I won't do that, no matter what the cost.'

Si. Harry had called her Si. Tears welled up and spilled over, to run down her cheeks and drip off her jaw. She liked that. 'I love you, Harrison Frost. I love you like I've never loved before. And won't ever again. You are the one.' She whispered these final sentences, afraid to say them too loud in case they ricocheted around the room for ever.

CHAPTER ELEVEN

HARRY PAUSED AT the gate in the fence they'd begun using this past week. Sienna was still talking. To him? Couldn't be. Had to be having a yarn with herself, or one of the Santas on her tree.

'Just like my dad.'

The pain and sadness wound around him, made him cross his arms to keep her away.

'Never stopping in one place long enough…'

Harry sank to his haunches, unable to stop listening when he knew he should. Eavesdropping wasn't gentlemanly. Or polite. But how did he turn off from that longing, that despair? He couldn't. Every word dug into him, twisted his gut tighter, smacked his heart. He understood her need for control; she had to hold on to what was around her, to keep her life on the straight and narrow. She believed she had her father's genes, but he didn't accept that. She was too grounded, just didn't know how to let go a little. Though these past two weeks she'd gone some way to achieving that.

He didn't want to hear any more. Sienna's sadness was too hard to deal with. It resonated with his. He leapt up and headed for his deck, where his shoulder slumped against an upright holding the roof above, the light drizzle he hadn't really noticed until now making the warm air heavy and his skin uncomfortable. As far as days went, this one had been a doozy. Make that, the worst in a long time. Confusion reigned supreme. Two jobs in two cities. The rescue position was his preference, even if permanent. Melbourne would be safer on his heart, but still filled with difficulties.

Both positions offered security in one way or another. Both would give him time to settle a bit, possibly buy a home, not a house to rent out to some ungrateful tenant. Both came fraught with problems—big problems. His family versus the woman who'd stolen his heart and wasn't letting go; who'd just tightened the hold over him.

Decisions, decisions. He didn't know where to start. So he wouldn't. He'd take his usual out and sleep on it, see what popped up in his mind when he woke in the morning.

He didn't wake, because he didn't go to sleep. At four thirty he crawled out of bed and pulled on running shorts and a grey singlet. The colour suited his mood. Downing a glass of water, he debated where to go for a run. The roads would be quiet but didn't appeal. There were beaches to choose from or the hills if he could be bothered driving for an hour first. Mission Bay won out. Handy and easy to negotiate the way around to the next bays. He could head straight into work afterwards. No need to return home and risk seeing Sienna outside.

The sun had begun its climb up the sky as he locked his vehicle and did some stretches, trying to ease the kinks gained during the restless night spent tossing and turning in bed.

Bed. Sienna. The two fit together perfectly, and gave him lots of memories he'd given up trying to banish. She was one stubborn woman who refused to go away, even when there were kilometres between them. What was he going to do about her? About them?

Crunch, crunch, crunch went his shoes on the wet sand. *Swish, swish* went the small waves as they unfurled at the edge of the tidal line. *Thump, thump* went his brain as he focused on nothing more than the beach ahead and getting to the end without thinking about Sienna.

Or which job to take.

Or settling down.

Or whether to become a monk and hide with a religious sect living on some mountain in a far-eastern country.

Splat. His foot had snagged a small log, tipping him sideways to land spread-eagled on the hard sand. Great. Just perfect. Concentrating on trying not to concentrate on Sienna had dumped him hard. His ankle throbbed. A cut on his hand from a shell trickled blood. Double great.

Sienna Burch, this is all your fault.

Scrambling to his feet, he tentatively tried out his ankle. A dull ache, and when he shifted his weight onto that leg it was good to go. After rinsing his hand in the salt water he started for the end of the beach again, this time jogging at a slower pace, not trying to outrun everything in his head.

Strange, but it was quieter in there now, as though acting calm made him calm. He breathed deep, lifted his eyes to take in the blue sky with a few clouds scudding around the top of Rangitoto Island. The harbour waters were tossing up small whitecaps, and pleasure craft were already heading out from downtown Auckland, no doubt aiming for the fishing grounds. Gulls squawked overhead before diving deep into the water.

He couldn't fault the place. At moments like this he felt at home.

Harry tripped, righted himself. At home? Get away. This was not the city he wanted to stop in to put roots down. So he'd made one decision. But then that negated the job on offer here. Didn't it? Returning to Melbourne wasn't exciting him either. This wasn't working. He turned and jogged back to his four-wheel drive and a towel. After wiping himself down, he threw on a shirt and crossed the road to a café for an early breakfast and lots of very strong coffee.

His phone rang loud in the near empty café. 'Hi, Derek'

'Connor's down with gastro. I'm switching crews around. Can you come in now?'

'On my way.' He'd shower at the base before pulling on the stuffy red suit that the kids adored. Funny, but they were easier to handle when he was dressed up as their favourite character. 'Can you put my coffee in a takeout mug, please?' he asked as he paid the guy behind the counter. 'Those eggs were delish.'

'Thanks. Come again.'

Harry took his change and the coffee and headed for his vehicle, a bounce in his step. The day ahead was sorted, leaving no time trying to find ways to fill in the hours.

All he had to do, and that wouldn't be until later, was to figure out why he was really holding out on spending more time with Sienna when he adored her and couldn't get enough of her. Not that she'd welcome him in her life with open arms. He would have to earn that right.

There were the 'don't want to be pushed around' and 'lack of trust' issues, but there was something else ticking at the back of all this. It rose whenever he considered the jobs he'd been offered. Again when he compared cities, and the friends he had through work in both those places. It always came back to Sienna and why he was afraid to love her.

Um…actually he already did love her.

That's why I can't decide. Holy moly.

He was stumped. Now what? It wasn't as though he could rush in and tell Sienna. She was too vulnerable, and their lifestyles were still poles apart. He swallowed the sudden pain gripping him. To admit his love to Sienna was impossible if he was to remain strong and invulnerable and not hurt her.

Why, damn it, why?

Sienna bounced back onto the ward on Monday morning feeling happy to be there and knowing she had other things to look forward to at the end of the day. 'Morning, Dale,' she smiled as she picked up patient notes from the desk. 'I've had the best break, thanks to you nagging.'

His face fell. 'We need to have a word. Grab a coffee and meet me in my office.'

Why did that sound ominous? A chill ran down her spine. 'You want one?'

'Already got it.' He started down the corridor in the opposite direction.

What was going on? Opting for a double-shot long black to keep the sense of unease at bay, she headed into Dale's office and at his instruction shut them in. The apprehension increased. 'You're freaking me out.'

'Do you remember Wendy Hall?'

'You took over from her about six months before I came on board.' Her reputation as a determined woman for getting her own way hadn't been kept quiet even after she'd gone.

'She's coming home from London next month and is making it known she wants her old job back.' Anger rode off Dale in waves. 'I have no intention of letting that happen. I am here for the long haul.'

So where did she fit into the picture? 'You think I need to be concerned for my job?'

'Yours is the next one up for renewal and somehow she knows that—I suspect from a certain board member she's always had under her thumb.'

Sienna slumped back in the chair. 'But I don't understand. Am I going to have to compete for my position?'

'It probably won't come to that. I'm just giving you warning so you can make sure you're up to speed with all the changes going on in the hospital.'

'I need to know what shifts the cleaners are doing now that their new contract has gone off-shore?' This was payback for having fun last week, for spreading her wings and living life outside of here. For *getting* a life. So much for planning how to use those other weeks' leave owing. She'd never use them now.

Dale balanced a pen between his thumbs. 'Not quite, but be on your toes all the time. Just in case.'

Just in case. Those words followed her around all day. She could lose her security, her sense of worth, her control—all because Wendy Hall wanted to take her job as a stepping stone on the way to the top. Just as well she had walked away from Harrison. There was no way she could fit into his lifestyle now. She needed to hold on to her job to know who she was. Didn't she?

Of course she had to hold on to this position. She worked too hard to let it go now just because someone else thought they could snatch it off her. Thank goodness for emergencies or she'd have hidden away and spent the rest of the day trying absorb that idea.

'Jonty Brooks is on his way down from the rescue chopper,' Julie told Sienna a little after three.

'Get the mask and oxygen set up in Room

Three.' Sienna flicked through the computer files until she had Jonty's before her. The six-year-old was a regular with severe asthma who lived on a remote island. 'He was in here last week with a severe attack.'

'Time of the year, I suppose,' Julie said. 'Here he is.'

Sienna looked up and directly at Harrison—dressed in an oversized red outfit with white fluff at the neck and cuffs. She smothered a laugh. 'Hello, Santa. How's Jonty today?'

'His condition's not as severe as it was last week, but he needs attention.' Harry handed her the patient notes he'd filled in. 'How's your first day back?'

Hell on wheels. 'Wish I'd stayed away.'

He stared at her. 'Never thought I'd hear you say that.'

She'd never thought so either. She shrugged and stepped up to the stretcher. 'Hi, Jonty. Hello, Mrs Brooks.' His mother looked tired, probably due to some major seasonal work happening on the farm. This family never stopped working, including all six children, right down to the five-year-old. Sometimes Sienna wondered if that contributed to Jonty's recurring asthma attacks, exhaustion taking away his ability to fight physical blows. The boy was pale despite spending most of his days outside. She'd add a CBC to his requirements while here to see if he was anaemic.

'Jonty had two minor attacks during the night apparently,' Harry, standing beside her, said quietly so as no one else heard. 'How minor is of concern. It took some time for the nebuliser to help his breathing.'

'The family's usually pretty good at calling for help if they're worried.' But once they'd been too busy with shearing and Jonty had been very ill that time. 'I'll look into it.'

'Good. I'll head away. The chopper's waiting.' But he didn't move.

Sienna looked at Harry properly, and had to bite down on the wave of need swamping her.

I miss him all the time.

No doubt about it. She loved him. And if she hadn't had two weeks off work it would never have happened. That was what came of stepping outside her comfort zone. 'Love the outfit,' she told him while thinking, would she do it again if she could go back to the night she came off her bike and rerun the days differently? Or would she turn up here every single day and work all the hours that came her way so as not to get thrown under a bus by Wendy Hall?

Flying had turned out to be one of the few things that she couldn't line up in straight lines all the time, wasn't in control of all the factors affecting flight or the engine or what other aircraft were sharing her space in the sky. And she loved it. Got so much pleasure from learning how to master a plane that she felt alive in a way she hadn't since she was a child going down to the river to catch eels with her dad. That hadn't stopped her doing school work. She'd done both. And coped, been more rounded than she'd become as an adult.

'Doctor?' Julie was waiting on the other side of the stretcher. 'We need to get Jonty offloaded onto a bed.'

Cripes. She'd been completely distracted. Harry had said he was on his way, in other words needed his stretcher back. 'Let's go.' Taking one corner, she began pushing the stretcher towards the room he'd be in. Jonty needed her concentrating on him, no one else.

In very little time the boy had been transferred and Harrison was taking his stretcher to the lift. Julie was listening to Jonty's chest and reading the monitors noting his heart activity.

'Give Jonty another corticosteroid injection, Julie. And then we monitor him. I'm also wondering if we might get a CBC and renal functions done in case there's an underlying illness going on.' A gut feeling there was more going on than what they were used to with Jonty had her tossing up other ideas and rejecting them.

'You think anaemia? Or worse?' Julie asked away from Mrs Brooks.

'Hopefully neither, but Jonty is paler than usual, and Harrison thought his previous two attacks might've been more severe than the family let on. I'm playing safe, really.' But listening to her gut had saved patients in the past. 'I'll talk you through my thoughts once we've got him stabilised.'

'Haemoglobin's nine-point-five,' Julie told her an hour later. 'Severe iron deficiency. Renal function normal.'

The lab had added iron studies after getting that haemoglobin result. 'Right, now we know what we're dealing with. All we have to do is find the cause.'

'At Jonty's age it'd be diet, wouldn't it? Or celiac disease.' Julie's brow creased in thought.

'Most likely, but we need to check for internal bleeding anyway. He could've been kicked in the stomach by a calf, though I'd have thought he'd have been brought in if that was the case.'

Thank goodness for busy. Knock-off time came around fast and for a minute Sienna tossed up whether to stay or to hand over to the night team. She was afraid of losing her job to Wendy Hall but the past two weeks had shown her more to life, and maybe she could take a chance on what the woman might do to her. What was the worst that could happen? Losing her job would break her heart but it wouldn't destroy her.

'This is where we're at with Jonty,' she told the head paediatrician coming on for the night shift. After running through the notes she walked away, fully expecting the roof to fall in on her.

By the time she pulled into her drive she was beginning to relax. Then she noticed Harry climbing out of his four-wheel drive and the tightness returned.

'How's Jonty?' he called over the fence.

After filling him in and trying to not gaze into his eyes like a lovelorn teenager she closed the garage and went inside to pour a wine. Yes, she'd decided one glass on her own wasn't going to turn her into an alcoholic.

There was a lot to think about, but instead she immersed herself in the theory of flight, and weather patterns.

Tuesday was busy with three serious admissions leaving little time for anything other than hastily downed lukewarm coffee at intermittent moments, but Sienna didn't hang around when it was obvious the staff didn't need her. By the time she got home all she wanted was to put her feet up and enjoy a wine while eating dinner and reading the flight training manual. It was her new passion. Not that it cancelled out the passion that was Harrison. Sussing out the apartment next door, looking for him, was not an option. But want to or not, she still did it. Often. Finally, to distract herself, she put the manuals aside and wrapped the few Christmas presents she'd bought a couple of weeks back and placed them under the tree, including one for Harry.

Staring at the green-and-red paper covering

the long, narrow box containing a fishing rod, she knew it was a mistake. He wouldn't drop by on Christmas Day. For one, he'd probably be in Melbourne, and two, even if he wasn't he wouldn't call in to see her ever again. She'd wrecked two chances, one more than most people got. But she hadn't been able to resist buying the rod. It had had his name on it. Of course, why she'd even gone into the hunting and fishing shop in the first place was a mystery.

Retrieving the parcel, she took it out to the garage and leaned it against the cupboard in a corner out of the way. Out of sight. Back in the lounge she sank into a chair and let the tears fall for a few minutes before straightening her back, plastering on a reluctant smile and turning on the TV. She could be happy. Her life was changing, not necessarily how she'd envisaged entirely, but one step at a time she'd make it work out.

Except for Wendy Hall creating waves, that was. Dale had set up a meeting with two board members, himself and Sienna that afternoon, and she felt more confident that they'd do all they could to renew her contract. When she'd suggested they draw it up a month early there'd been some hesitation, so she'd had to drop the idea. But what was bothering her more than anything was that she wasn't losing sleep over the whole idea of her job being in jeopardy.

Not that she was planning on going hooking up with Harrison and traipsing around after him. He'd have to love her for her to do that, and there'd been no sign of love coming from him.

Wednesday brought Santa to the ward, handing out presents and good cheer, and generally causing mayhem with the kids. Sienna watched the excitement with a lump in her throat and a knot in her heart. She wanted this. Kids, presents, Santa, the whole shebang.

With Harrison. In Melbourne? Or Auckland? Or the back of beyond? No, she hadn't progressed that far.

Her smile slipped. She pulled it back, getting used to wearing one even when she felt like curling up in a ball and crying. When a little boy rushed up to her waving the toy aeroplane he'd unwrapped, Sienna got down on her knees and played flying games with him. 'This is the best medicine out,' she told Julie.

'We should bottle it,' Julie replied as she worked to remove sticky goop from a toddler's hair. 'Though I'd be leaving this stuff out.'

That night Sienna and Anna hit the town for cocktails followed by dinner to celebrate the season as they did every year. 'To us.' Sienna knocked her glass against her friend's after they'd been yakking for a while.

Anna took a large mouthful of her drink, looking as though she was about to cry. 'To another Christmas without husbands and kids.'

'Whoa. Where did that come from?' Shock rippled through Sienna. Anna never sounded sad about her lot. Angry, sometimes, yes, even nostalgic, but sad?

'Did you hear yourself when you were talking about your day on the ward? Did you feel the longing that was in your voice when you mentioned those kids and their excitement? We are missing out on all that.'

No denying she'd felt it earlier in the day, but Sienna hadn't realised it was still in her system, and worse, had let her yearning rise to the fore. 'Sure we are, but we're also living how we choose.' Harrison appeared behind her eyes, and he was waving, like she needed reminding of her love for him and how she'd like that to unfold.

'We're both so tied up in our careers I sometimes wonder how we function in the real world.'

'Who ticked you off today?' This so wasn't her friend talking.

'Your Felicity's making me take a look at myself. She's gutsy and determined to get ahead with school and friends and everything that comes her way despite the cystic fibrosis ruling her life. She never stops talking about you and how wonderful you are, yet she only knows half the picture.'

'My Felicity? She's a patient I've got to know well over the years and am trying to help in other ways than medical.'

'Of course. Nothing to do with your loving side, your need to be engaged with people, your caring nature.' Finally Anna's smile was back in place, and she sipped her mojito. 'You going to do anything about Mr Sexy?'

The warmth drained from her face. 'We're not really talking at the moment.'

'You should do something about that. Don't let the problem get so big it can't be managed.'

If only it were that simple. 'No point. Harry heads home to Australia in a couple of days.' Which had to be a good thing, right? He wouldn't take the position at the rescue base. Permanent wasn't a word in his vocabulary.

'Damn it, Sienna, stop making everything so hard. Take some risks, have some fun.'

'Oh, like you do, right?'

'Well, one of us has to break the mould first. Why not you?'

Good question, and one that kept blinking on in the front of her mind for the rest of the evening, and all through the night, and on the way to work next morning. Unfortunately, an answer wasn't so quick or determined to make itself known. Or was she hiding from it? Afraid of the consequences of taking further risks?

'There you go, sport.' Harry nodded farewell to the thirteen-year-old lad the rescue helicopter had just delivered to North Shore Hospital. 'Take care. No more riding your cycle on one wheel over the cliff onto the beach ten metres below.' Luck had been on the kid's side. His arm was broken but otherwise nothing more serious than a few bruises. About as lucky as Si had been.

Si. He wished he could stop calling her that. The abbreviated version of Sienna had slipped into his vocabulary one day and refused to disappear. Si meant warmth, excitement, hurt, longing. And a load more.

Including taking the biggest risk of his adult life.

Connor sat opposite him in the chopper and reached for his safety harness. 'What time's your flight out?'

'Midnight.'

'Want to have a farewell drink with the gang before you go?'

A farewell drink. 'Probably not. I've got to see Derek, and then there are some things I have to do at the apartment before I head away.'

The look he received from over the top of Connor's sunglasses told him he'd let his friends down, but it couldn't be helped. There were more important details to attend to. He could only hope everyone would understand when it became general knowledge on the base. 'I'll put some money on the bar.'

'Wish you were hanging around.'

Harry's eyes widened. 'Thanks. It's been a good number, this one.'

Connor got busy writing up case notes, leaving Harry to contemplate his navel. He checked his phone. No messages. Sienna was still cold on him. Like he'd done anything to crank up their relationship. The time read five forty-two. By the time the chopper landed and they'd restocked the kits it would be knock-off time. His final stint over and done with. Auckland had been a lark. The job one of the best. The people—he'd made some good friends he'd miss.

He tapped the photo icon and up came all the reasons he should stay. Sienna laughing at his Christmas tree. Sienna winding in her first snapper. Sienna sound asleep on the outdoor couch in the shade at the bach in Coromandel. Sienna—

Tap. Stop it.

'You won't change your mind about leaving?' Connor asked, a guarded expression on his face.

Did he know there was a position on offer? It was a small base and word got around fast at times, though Derek said no one knew his plans. But that wasn't the question. Would he change his mind? He looked out at the harbour below and the rapidly approaching city centre with the ferries at the quays, the workers on their way home or to the bars. The Sky Tower where he'd challenged Sienna into agreeing they should leap off and take a chance on a piece of rope. Should he remind her they had yet to see that through? What was the point when they weren't about to become an item? But if he stayed they might. Might not, either.

What did he have to lose by staying? His heart was already entrenched here, and his chance at a future that included family and roots and friendships he wasn't always walking away from was also here.

What did he have to lose by leaving? All of the above.

Man, oh, man. Just like that, he knew. Harry leaned forward. 'Thanks, mate.'

'Pay me later.' There was a small smile twitching at the man's mouth.

Harry squirmed in his seat, stretched his legs out, drew them up again, folded his arms around his waist, dropped them onto his thighs. It never took this long to reach base.

'I'll do the stock,' Connor announced as they

finally dropped out of the chopper right outside the main hangar.

Was he that easy to read? 'Thanks, again.'

The day had dragged. Gone was the small spring in Sienna's steps, gone was the enthusiasm for everything. That there were fewer admissions only added to her gloom. 'It's as though people are refusing to get sick because of Christmas.' Hopefully no one was staying away when it was imperative they see a doctor.

Once Sienna was away from the ward and back at home changing out of her work clothes into shorts and a tee shirt, Christmas loomed larger than ever in her mind. Unheard of. It rattled her stoic, professional front. Her mother and Bill had arrived early yesterday and promptly taken over her kitchen. Nothing unusual there, except for the tingle of excitement sneaking under her radar. The traditions set in place over the last few years were claiming her as never before. Previously she'd held on to them as a way of keeping the past out of the way. This year they gave hope for the future, and yet she couldn't see how that would really change the way she'd like it to. They certainly didn't include Harrison—or those children she wanted to have.

There were the same number of presents under the tree. She wasn't counting the one languishing out in the garage. That would go to a charity shop in the new year.

Harrison seemed to be out all the time. If his attire of those in-your-face overalls were anything to go by, he'd made himself available for every shift. His body had been slumped with exhaustion as he'd walked up the drive half an hour ago. Presumably he'd be heading to the airport any time soon to catch a flight home.

So you're going to let him go without a word?

She was hardly going to attempt to get onside with him a third time. She might be a novice at the dating game, but she wasn't entirely stupid. She understood it wasn't working between them, and that there were too many reasons why it never would.

Yes, and you are one of the biggest reasons. Gasp. What?

You're afraid.

Yes, she sure was. Unwilling to take more

risks than she'd already managed. Didn't want to end up being her mother, never settling when it was her greatest wish, all because of love.

But you're more than willing for Harrison to stop moving from a job he enjoys to another he'll enjoy just so you can be happy.

Was she being selfish? Harry didn't know she loved him. She had no real idea what he felt for her; guessing games didn't cut it. There was risk number one, laying her heart on the line without knowing the outcome.

Third time lucky.

Now, where did that come from? He was leaving. Better he knew the truth than have him go away totally unaware she loved him.

'Sienna?'

'Yes, Mum?'

'Is that man in the other apartment the one you had such a wonderful time with in Coromandel?'

'He sure is.'

Her mother's sigh had Sienna turning to stare at her. 'Mum.'

'Just remembering, that's all.'

'Dad?'

'Yes. It wasn't all bad, you know.'

'You two used to tuck me up in bed and go walking, hand in hand along the beach or the river bank or whatever was there. I'd follow sometimes and you were completely oblivious to anything but yourselves, laughing, talking, kissing.' She'd forgotten those times.

'You followed us?' Her mother's face coloured up. 'How often?'

'Often enough. Relax. I always knew when it was time to disappear back to my bed.' Suddenly the hesitation was gone. She and Harrison had shared some wonderful days and nights. It hadn't only been about the lovemaking, but all the conversations and laughter, and the fishing. Togetherness. It had been the best two days of her adult life. And she wanted more of them. Would Harrison? With her? Only one way to find out.

But first she'd brush her hair out the way he liked it, and put on that blue blouse he liked so much. Cosmetic changes, sure, but why not? This was the man she loved and would do anything for. Anything? Yes, anything.

She snagged a bottle of wine on the way through the kitchen.

* * *

Harry saw Sienna coming up from her apartment as he headed down his drive. They met at the letterboxes, each with a bottle of wine in their hands. That had to be a good sign. 'Hey,' he said.

'Hey, yourself.' She didn't hesitate, or blush; her eyes didn't turn frosty. She kept on coming, her empty hand reaching out to him. 'I wanted to see you before you left.' Then she stumbled. 'There are things I need to tell you.'

Catching her, Harry slipped his fingers through hers and held tight. 'I was on my way to tell you I'm not leaving.'

Her head jerked upward, her gaze searching his face before finally locking onto his eyes. 'You're not?' Some emotion made her voice squeaky. He thought it might be hope. Or that could be wishful thinking on his part. Sienna swallowed hard and tried again. 'You're not going back to Melbourne tonight?'

'Not tonight, not for a long time, other than briefly to visit my brothers and friends in a few weeks' time.'

'Where, then?' she whispered.

'I'm staying here. I've accepted the base director's post. It's a job I'd like to own, to be able to make changes as I see fit, train more volunteers and look after the paid staff.'

Her fingers were gripping his. 'Wow. That's quite a change of direction for you.' He could almost fall into her eyes, they were so large. 'Glad I brought the wine.'

'You want to celebrate me hanging around to annoy you?'

'Is that what you intend doing?' She was holding her breath, as though the next thing he told her would be the most important ever. Was she aware her fingernails were digging into his palm?

'If you'll let me.' Then Harry couldn't breathe either. Had to be something in the air to be affecting them both in the same way.

Damn but he was a fool. But he wasn't used to opening up his heart.

Just do it. Put it out there. Deep, deep breath.

'Sienna, I love you. I didn't want to. I fought it hard, but there was no stopping you getting into my heart. You're changing me, making me stand up for those things I have been denying I want for so long.' There was no stopping him now he'd started. It was as if a cloud had finally evaporated, to be replaced by sunshine. 'I want the whole caboodle with you. Love, laughter, tears if we have to, kids, even. What do you think?' His chest hurt as air stalled in his lungs. If she didn't answer him fast he might drop in a heap at her feet, gasping like a fish on the sand.

She tried to pull away, but he increased the pressure to keep contact. 'Tell me,' he said with as much constraint as possible.

'I...' Sienna paused, looked around them and returned to watching him. 'I want you to know our weekend away was extra-special and I'd like to repeat it. Not necessarily doing the same things in the same place, but repeating the togetherness.'

Harry's heart beat hard against his ribs. 'I hear you. I even agree. But—' A finger from the hand holding that bottle pressed his lips, effectively shutting him up.

'I've gone and fallen in love with you.' Her eyes lightened, and that mouth that could do wonders on his skin curved upwards. 'I love you, Harrison. End of story.'

Knots in his stomach and around his heart dropped away. A weight lifted from him. 'Or the beginning of a whole new one.'

That smile widened. 'I didn't want to push my luck saying that.' Then she stared at him, her finger now worrying *her* lips.

Wrapping his arms around her waist, he picked her up and swung them around in a circle. 'We'd better not drop the bottles. We've got some celebrating to do.' Then, placing her on her feet, he proceeded to kiss her until he lost all cohesive thought, only Sienna stealing into his mind.

Then she pulled back. 'There are some problems on the horizon. I might lose my job due to someone wanting to use it to get to the top in a hurry, but I think I can live with that if you're with me.' She hesitated, doubt beginning to fill her eyes, darken her face. 'In fact, I wouldn't mind less hours at work if it meant doing other interesting things.'

'All the way, sweetheart.'

'I've learned that I'm ready to take some chances, to let go some of my hang-ups—all because of you. To the point that—' she locked her eyes with his '—I will go wherever you want to go. I no longer need to stop in one place for ever, Harry, as long as I can be with you.'

'I won't ask you to do that.' As she started to

say something he held up a finger. 'I am stopping running away. Yes, that's what I've been doing for so long now it's a habit, a bad one that needs banishing.' Swallow.

'Don't be rash. There might be times you want, need, to move on. Take your version of a road trip. I'll be there with you.'

Then Harry knew what to do. Reaching for her free hand that had got away from him, his fingers slid between hers again as naturally as opening his eyes when he woke in the morning. 'Come with me. I'll show you the only road trip we're doing.' Turning her around, he tugged her down his drive and back up hers, around the corner to her back yard and onto her deck, where he gently pushed her down onto a chair before pulling another close and sitting beside her. Then twisted the lid off his bottle of wine and held it up. 'This is what we'll drink to. Our way of keeping the world moving at our pace, keeping us safe from the past and moving into the future.' He nodded at the two magnificent rhododendrons. 'Together we will watch those trees grow bigger and stronger.'

Sienna squealed and leapt up. 'You're serious.'

'Very.' He placed the bottle on the nearby

table before it was knocked out of his grasp as Sienna clambered onto his lap, her legs on either side of his thighs, her hands taking his head and drawing him close for a kiss. A kiss that ignited every point in his body and fused his brain until he knew nothing but Sienna.

Until, 'Oh, dear. I think this is the moment we disappear, Bill. I'm not going to bed, like Si used to do, but I think we need to buy some more pine nuts for that salad I'm planning on making.'

Who the hell...? Harry pulled his mouth away from that kiss and stared over Sienna's shoulder at an older version of his woman. She looked very amused about something. No doubt them kissing. The older man at her side wore the same expression. Oh, boy. Talk about caught. Why this sensation of being a naughty teen snogging the girl from class? Kissing his woman was allowed. Yeah, but not in front of her mother before he'd even met her.

As Sienna wriggled around on his lap, nudging that obvious reaction to her kiss and causing him more distress, he went for light-hearted and silly. 'Hi, I'm Harry Frost. Sienna's neighbour. Do you think you could get me a packet of…?' *Not condoms.* 'Um…a box of chocolates while you're there?'

Sienna gasped out a laugh. 'Guess we're even, Mum.'

The lovely woman stepped forward, her hand out to him. 'I know exactly who you are, Mr Neighbour. I'm Katie, Sienna's mother.' As her warm hand wrapped around the one he hadn't realised he'd put out she nodded to the man with her. 'This is my friend Bill.'

Still with Sienna on his lap, though now facing her mother and hopefully hiding the bulge she'd caused, he shook Bill's hand too. 'I'm glad to meet you both.'

Katie laughed that light, tinkling sound he knew from Sienna. 'I doubt that very much, Harry. Timing is everything and you've got it a bit messed up tonight. So, which brand of chocolates shall I get?' Even her eyes twinkled like Si's. 'I think we'll walk to the supermarket, Bill. That should fill in time before dinner,' she spun back to Harry, 'which you're invited to, by the way.'

Did he tell her he could just take Sienna next door for that hour to continue what had to be finished or he'd combust with need, and that no one had to go shopping for things they didn't require? Somehow that might earn him a swipe across the arm from the younger version of the woman standing before him.

The younger one was speaking up. 'Do I get to say anything?'

'Nope,' replied her mother. 'Not a word. See you shortly.'

'Not too shortly,' Harry whispered in Sienna's ear, and yep, got the swipe on his arm.

'I'll get the glasses and we can take them back to your side of the fence. Just in case we forget to stop whatever we're getting up to in time.'

EPILOGUE

CHRISTMAS DAY DAWNED bright and clear. Just like her head and heart, Sienna mused as she stood under the shower. Harrison's shower. Last night they'd made it over to her apartment for dinner with her mother and Bill, and spent a couple of hours chatting and laughing. Lots of laughing, actually. Most unusual. And wonderful…freeing.

'You going to use all the hot water?' The shower door swung open and Harry stepped in. He filled his hands from the liquid-soap dispenser and rubbed it over her shoulders, down to her breasts. 'Merry Christmas, sweetheart.'

'Same back at you.' She kissed his chin, his cheek, then his mouth, hunger rampant in an instant.

As it very obviously was in Harry. Leaning against him, she rubbed her belly across that hot reaction, needing him in her—again.

Harry pulled his mouth away. 'We probably

shouldn't. We were expected for breakfast five minutes ago.'

'You don't do quick?' Her hand wrapped around him.

'Oh, yeah. Watch me.'

'I think you mean feel me.' And before she knew it her body was falling apart under the onslaught of heat and need.

Within minutes they were towelling themselves dry, grinning at each other as if they'd just unwrapped the best Christmas present ever. Which she had. 'Harry, thank you for being you.'

When he reached for her, that level of intensity in his eyes spelling more passion, she ducked away. 'We really should to go next door.' And there was another present she had to put under the tree. 'Mum will be clock-watching.'

But her mother surprised her. 'Coffee's just made. I thought we could open presents while we have that. Breakfast will be thirty minutes.' She looked from Sienna to Harrison and back again, the acceptance of him warm in her eyes, and adding to Sienna's glow. 'I allowed extra time for you to get here.'

'Thanks, Mum,' she growled around a swallowed laugh. She and her mother didn't talk about things like this. But other than Bernie, whom Mum hadn't liked, there hadn't been men in her life to talk about. And now there was. The most wonderful man she'd known. 'Harry, can you pour the coffee? I've got something to get from the garage.'

The fishing rod was a hit. 'Does this mean we're going to Coromandel again?' Harry asked with a grin. 'You won't grump about smelling like something the cat left in the back of the cupboard last week?'

'Of course I will. And I'll get you to gut the fish I catch so I don't stink for a week.' That grin drove her crazy. If her mother and Bill weren't here she'd be dragging Harry down the hall to her bedroom right now. Christmas breakfast or not.

Harrison handed her an envelope, and sat back waiting, his eyes full of amusement.

'What?' Slipping her finger under the flap, she opened it and tipped out the card inside. And swallowed. 'The bungee jump. I was hoping you'd forgotten about that.'

'A challenge was made and accepted.' He grinned. 'You're not chickening out, are you?'

Unfortunately not. 'Don't push your luck.'

Harry laughed. 'You'll enjoy it, sweetheart.'

'I hope so.' Then she relaxed. She'd be fine. So far everything she'd done on her list had worked out. Why wouldn't this challenge? 'Bring it on.'

'Only if you want to.'

'Contrition doesn't suit you, Harry Frost.'

'Right, are we done?' Her mother looked under the tree. 'Who are these for?' She prodded the last three parcels.

'Anna, Fliss, who is a young friend working for Anna, and I don't know about the other one,' Sienna answered.

Harrison stood up and reached down for the red square packet with a huge gold satin ribbon. Then he dropped to one knee in front of her. 'For you, Si.' He held on to it. 'But first, I need to ask you something.'

Thud, thud. He'd better shout it because her ears were deafened by the pounding of her heart. 'Harry?'

'If we're going to watch those trees grow and raise some kids, and settle in one place, do you think we should get married to start the whole thing off?'

Her mother clapped.

Bill chuckled.

And Sienna—well, her eyes filled up and tears streamed down her cheeks. 'Absolutely,' she croaked. 'No other way to go.'

Then she was being wrapped in her favourite arms and kissed thoroughly.

In the background she thought she heard her mother laughing as she said, 'You'd better be quick. I'm not putting off breakfast for a second time.'

* * * * *

LET'S TALK

Romance

For exclusive extracts, competitions
and special offers, find us online:

f facebook.com/millsandboon

◎ @millsandboonuk

𝕏 @millsandboon

Or get in touch on 0844 844 1351*

For all the latest titles coming soon,
visit millsandboon.co.uk/nextmonth

*Calls cost 7p per minute plus your phone company's price per
minute access charge

Want even more
ROMANCE?

Join our bookclub today!